AN INSPECTOR HENRY TIBBETT MYSTERY

WHO IS SIMON WARWICK?

Patricia Moyes

An Owl Book

HENRY HOLT AND COMPANY
New York

Henry Holt and Company, Inc.
Publishers since 1866
115 West 18th Street
New York, New York 10011

Henry Holt® is a registered trademark
of Henry Holt and Company, Inc.

Published by Henry Holt and Company, Inc.,
115 West 18th Street, New York, New York 10011.

Library of Congress Cataloging-in-Publication Data
Moyes, Patricia.
Who is Simon Warwick?
I. Title.
PZ.M938Wh   1978   [PR6063.09]   823'.9'14   78-53951
ISBN 0-8050-0719-9 (An Owl Book: pbk.)

Henry Holt books are available for special promotions
and premiums. For details contact:
Director, Special Markets.

First published in hardcover by
Holt, Rinehart and Winston in 1978.

First Owl Book Edition—1982

Printed in the United States of America
9   10   8

For Helen and Charles Marwick

1

A rainy November night in London. Roads like black satin ribbons, reflecting restless pools of bright lamplight, and the shifting, stabbing beams of car headlights. In the small streets behind Belgrave Square, a few scurrying pedestrians under black umbrellas, a few dark-suited men trying to hail taxis, while their pale-chiffon ladies shiver under the inadequate protection of neo-classical porticoes; a few cars—like cats, all black in the dark—making their hesitant, rain-blinded way on the slippery tarmac.

Ambrose Quince, peering at the street ahead through the metronome-swish of windshield wipers, thought longingly of his snug drawing room in Ealing, of a mellow Scotch and soda, and of his wife, Rosalie, warm and supple in a silky housecoat, her bare feet tucked under her as she sat on the floor in front of the log fire. Ordinarily, he would have been home an hour ago; but, on this filthy evening, the telephone had had to ring just as he was leaving the office in Theobald's Road. Miss Benedict, his secretary, had announced that Lord Charlton's office wished to speak with him, and shortly afterward an authoritative male voice had informed him that Lord Charlton would be grateful if Mr. Quince would wait upon him at his London residence at eight-thirty. It was in connection with His Lordship's will, so Mr. Quince would be kind enough to bring the document with him. Thank you very much, Mr. Quince.

Well, a modestly situated solicitor in his late thirties does not hestitate when his only really important client requests his presence, even at eight-thirty on a December night. He makes it his business to be there, even with bad grace. In fact, Ambrose knew very well that he was extremely lucky to have retained even a small part of Lord Charlton's business. It was a sentimental gesture on the old man's part, a recognition of the days when Ambrose's father and three uncles had formed the law firm of Quince, Quince, Quince and Quince, and when His Lordship had still been plain Alexander Warwick, a pushy young businessman with unorthodox ideas. By now, Ambrose was the only Quince in the establishment that bore his name fourfold. His current partners—Mr. Rudley and Mr. Silverstein—were not, if one faced up to it, really very good. Ambrose, in his own mind, felt that he himself could have been good if he had had enough interesting cases to hold his attention. As it was, the firm jogged along, minimally efficient and completely uninspired; and Alexander Warwick—now Lord Charlton, the textile millionaire—provided a steady income by confiding his most personal but least important affairs to the last of the Quinces.

Lord Charlton's will, which now reposed in Ambrose's briefcase on the empty passenger seat of the car, was a document that had caused Ambrose many headaches in its time. Charlton was a bachelor, and his only brother and sister-in-law had both been killed by a German flying bomb that hit their London home near the end of the Second World War. With no close relatives or dependents, Lord Charlton had decided to leave his fortune to charity, apart from a few bequests to personal staff. This was not so much from a desire to help the worthy causes concerned, as from a determination that the collateral branches of the family should not lay their hands on a single penny. As a young man, Alexander Warwick had experienced nothing but hostility from his family, and he remembered his uncles and aunts with particular dislike. It infuriated him to think that their children's children might now have some legal claim on the money that he had worked so hard to amass. Ambrose's job was to provide a list of suitable charities as legatees, to set up a foundation to administer the money after Lord Charlton's death, and to make sure that the wording of the will itself was legally impeccable. As far as he knew, he had succeeded. He wondered what the trouble was now.

Twenty-one, Belgrave Terrace, was an imposing house on a quiet but piercingly expensive street near Hyde Park Corner.

2

Ambrose drove his three-year-old Ford up to the front door, got out under the shelter of the portico, and rang the bell. At once the door was opened by a courteous butler, who requested the car keys so that the footman might park the car in the mews behind the house. His Lordship was expecting Mr. Quince, and was in the library. If Mr. Quince would kindly step this way . . . ?

The house was very quiet. No traffic noise permeated those thick Georgian walls, and the pale Wedgwood-green carpet muffled Ambrose's footsteps. A French marble clock in the hallway chimed the half-hour with a thin, silver note. The butler opened a door, said, "Mr. Quince, Your Lordship," and stood back to let Ambrose enter the room.

Where the hall had been white and pale green, the library was brown and crimson. Floor-to-ceiling mahogany bookcases, stacked with leather-bound volumes; well-worn, comfortable leather armchairs; deep-red Persian rugs matching the velvet curtains; a great fireplace with the remains of two huge logs dissolving softly into glowing embers.

From one of the armchairs, a voice said, "Come in, Ambrose. Sit down."

"Thank you, Lord Charlton. Good evening, Lord Charlton."

Clutching his briefcase, Ambrose sat down in the chair on the far side of the fireplace. Every time he came to this house, he was determined not to be overawed by the old man. After all, what was Charlton but an opportunist who had made a fortune by getting into the synthetic-fabric market just ahead of his rivals? Nevertheless, there was something about the man. Something about the house. Ambrose could not deny it, even if he resented it.

He became aware that Charlton was looking at him steadily. The craggy face seemed thinner than usual, and more deeply lined. A trick of the flickering firelight, probably.

Ambrose said, "I believe there's something about your will, Lord Charlton. I have it here . . ."

Charlton did not appear to hear him. He sighed, then smiled and said, "Your father and I were good friends, Ambrose."

There did not seem to be a suitable reply, so Ambrose said nothing. Charlton went on, "I look forward to meeting him again."

This time, Ambrose did a small double-take. His father had been dead for eight years. Charlton, watching Quince's face, said, "Yes. You're quite right. The doctor told me today. Six months at the outside. So . . ." Suddenly the old man stood up, became brisk.

3

"So there's no time to waste. We must get working on that will."

"Working, Lord Charlton?" Ambrose was on his feet, heartily thankful that Charlton's sudden switch of mood made it unnecessary for him to proffer condolences. "I thought you were quite satisfied with the will, sir. We went through the list of charities together only last—"

"No, no, no." Charlton spoke quietly but decisively. "I am changing my will entirely. Everything I possess is to be left to my nephew."

"To your—?" Ambrose Quince sat down again, abruptly.

"Did you not know that I have a nephew? At least, I hope I have."

"No, Lord Charlton, I didn't."

"I also, apparently, have a conscience. Interesting, isn't it, Ambrose? I only discovered it this afternoon, after the doctor left. If I am to look your father in the eye, wherever it is that we may meet again, I shall have to account to him for what I did not do. I shall—" He paused. Then, "I see that all this comes as news to you. I thought that your father might have—but no, of course he wouldn't. He was far too discreet. Well, then, I had better explain. You know, don't you, Ambrose, that there was only one member of my family who was close to me—whom I loved?"

"I have heard . . . your brother . . ."

"That's right. My young brother Dominic. He married Mary Cheverton during the war—1943, it must have been. A very beautiful and charming girl. They had a little boy, you know. Not very long before they were killed in that flying-bomb attack."

Ambrose said, "They were all killed."

Lord Charlton, who was leaning against the mantelpiece gazing into the fire, suddenly turned to face Quince. "No," he said. And again, "No." There was a long pause. "It was given out later . . . we let it be understood . . . that the baby had died with them. That's not true. The baby survived."

"Then what on earth—?" Ambrose began.

Charlton silenced him with a small gesture. "Your father," he said, "got in touch with me at once. The baby had been taken to a children's hospital. Bobby Quince told me that I should adopt the child. I was the only living relative, you see."

"Was there nobody on the mother's side who—!"

Charlton smiled, a little grimly. "Nobody who wanted to know. Dominic Warwick was considered ill bred, a wastrel and maybe

4

worse. So was I, you must remember, Ambrose. It's only quite recently that I have become respectable. Mary Cheverton—the Honorable Mary Cheverton—was cut off with the proverbial shilling when she married my brother. No, I was the only person the little fellow had in the world—and I refused him."

"Why?" Ambrose had not intended to ask the question, but it came out of its own accord, and hung for a moment, unanswered.

Then Charlton said, "Who knows? Ostensibly, I was too busy. I had no wife, I was no fit person to look after a small baby. I had just begun to make money, and I wanted complete mobility, complete independence. Do you understand that?" There was an appeal in his voice.

Ambrose had no difficulty in replying. "I understand it absolutely, sir."

"Besides," added Charlton, "there was old Humberton."

"Old Humberton?"

"A solicitor. Friend of your father's. Practiced in Marstone, down on the south coast. He'd arranged some private adoptions during the war, and it seems he told your father that he could fix up young Simon—that was the baby's name, Simon—that he could arrange for Simon to be adopted by a very eligible young couple. An American army officer and his English bride. The girl had some sort of female internal trouble . . . could never have children of her own. The husband had been wounded in Normandy, and they were due for repatriation to the States in a matter of days. They wanted to take the baby with them." Another pause. "It seemed suitable. I agreed. And that was the end of Simon Warwick—until this afternoon."

Ambrose Quince swallowed, and said, "Well, sir, if you want to trace your nephew, you'll have to contact Mr. Humberton and get the name of the adoptive parents. Then—"

Charlton had walked over to the sideboard. He interrupted to say, "Whiskey or brandy, Ambrose?"

"Whiskey, if your please, sir. With water."

Charlton poured two whiskeys, added water, and carried them across the room to Ambrose Quince. "Here," he said.

"Thank you, sir. Your good health, sir." The words came out automatically, before he could stop them. He became aware that he was going very red in the face.

Charlton looked at him with a sardonic smile. He said, "We have already discussed my health, Ambrose. Of course, the doctor has told me that I mustn't drink spirits. One small glass of wine a day, perhaps. Otherwise, I am likely to die even sooner than predicted. Well, the few weeks of grace are not worth it." He raised his glass. "To *your* health, Ambrose. To my death."

Ambrose looked at his feet and mumbled something about being sorry.

"Nothing to be sorry for, for heaven's sake. The thing to do now is to find my nephew Simon."

"Well, sir, as I was saying—"

"No. No use. Humberton himself died five years ago, and his firm died with him. Papers relating to living and active clients at the time of his death were returned to them. All others, as far as I have been able to ascertain, were destroyed."

"But how—?"

Lord Charlton smiled, and lit a large and aromatic cigar. "Another pleasure prohibited by the medical profession. I must say, it gives a man a great sense of release to be beyond the aid of doctors." He took a leisurely puff. "Yes, some of my other lawyers have been investigating Humberton this afternoon. You must know that I employ other lawyers, Ambrose."

"Of course, sir."

"They did the footwork," said Charlton smoothly. "You can take it from me that nothing connected with the late Alfred Humberton will lead us any closer to Simon Warwick. In my dealings with Humberton over the adoption, he referred to the American couple as Captain and Mrs. X. I believe this is usual. The child is supposed to start life with a new identity, and no connection with his previous family."

Ambrose said, "It's a very strange story, sir."

"Strange? What d'you mean, strange?"

"Well . . . a private adoption arranged by a lawyer in a matter of a few days . . . and to a foreign couple who were taking the baby out of the country. I don't see how the formalities could have—"

"The war, my dear boy. The war. You're too young to remember. A lot of people sent their small children across the Atlantic to avoid the air raids during the blitz, and the rocket attacks set off a new exodus. Many of the children traveled alone, with labels on their coats, to be picked up by relatives or friends on the other side."

"They still needed passports," said Ambrose.

"Yes, of course. My inquiries have led me that far. A British

6

passport was issued to the infant Simon Warwick in 1944. Presumably that was the document with which he entered the United States."

"So he was not officially adopted when he left England?"

"Apparently not. The formalities must have been concluded in America. I never heard any more about it, from Humberton or anybody else. I regret to say that at the time it was a great weight off my mind. But now . . ." Lord Charlton sat down slowly, like the old man he was. "First of all, let's get that new will drafted."

"But, sir—"

"Don't argue with me, Ambrose. Just get out pen and paper, and we'll do it in no time. I, Alexander Warwick, Baron Charlton, being of sound mind et cetera, do give and bequeath—got that?"

"Yes, sir, but—"

"Do give and bequeath all my worldly possessions . . . goods and chattels . . . whatever the legal mumbo-jumbo is, you fill that in, Ambrose, I mean *everything* . . . to my nephew Simon Warwick. That's simple enough, isn't it?"

A near groan from Ambrose Quince indicated that it was far from simple. "Lord Charlton . . . I beg you . . . surely you must find the young man first and alter the will afterwards?"

"Certainly not. I've told you, Ambrose, the doctor remarked with some relish that I might drop dead at any moment. Change that will, and find Simon for me."

"How, Lord Charlton?"

"I don't know what's the matter with you, Ambrose. Perfectly simple. Start off by drafting an advertisement, which you will run in all prominent newspapers, both here and in the United States. Start with the name, in block capitals. 'SIMON WARWICK. Will Simon Warwick, only son of Dominic and Mary (née Cheverton) Warwick, get in touch with Messrs. Quince and Quince and—however many there are of you. Will hear something to his advantage.' What's difficult about that?"

"Lord Charlton," Ambrose said, "the boy . . . the man . . . he must be in his thirties by now . . . the man won't know who he is. I mean, who he was. The name Simon Warwick will mean nothing to him."

"We can't be sure, Ambrose. Humberton, quite rightly, never told me the identity of the new parents, but they knew whose son they were adopting. They may have told him. More likely, they'll see the advertisement themselves. And then, as you so rightly pointed out, there was that childhood passport in the name of Simon Warwick. It's perfectly possible that somewhere, in some American suburb, there lives a rising young executive who knows very well that he is Simon Warwick, and who will turn up with that passport to prove it. I want him. I want him here, if possible before I die."

"I begin to see," Ambrose said, forgetting his diffidence. "It's the business, isn't it? You're facing the prospect of dying without being able to keep the business in the family."

Charlton gave him a sharp look. "You are bright, young man," he said. "If you hadn't been, I would never have employed you, father or no father. Very well. I've outlined your job. Change the will—I shall expect it for signature tomorrow. Then find Simon Warwick for me. It will be worth your while, I can assure you."

"Look, sir," said Ambrose. "There's something I simply have to say."

"What's that?"

"Well . . . if you . . . if we put those ads in the papers, we're going to attract a whole lot of frauds."

"Frauds?"

"Once you put in the words 'something to his advantage,' you attract their interest. Crooks, I mean. Adventurers. Then, you want to print the name, Simon Warwick. It's not difficult for anybody to connect that up with you, and the Charlton fortune. Somerset House will produce a copy of the birth certificate for anybody." Ambrose sighed. "I'm afraid we may be saddled with quite a few pseudo Simon Warwicks, sir."

Lord Charlton said, "Don't worry about that, Ambrose."

"Sir, I think we must worry. In the absence of proper documentation, if somebody turns up with a plausible story . . ."

"I told you not to worry."

"I mean, there's a great deal of money at stake—"

Charlton turned and looked at Ambrose Quince. He said, "I shall know my brother's son when I meet him."

"Of course, there's such a thing as a family resemblance, but I don't see how you can possibly rely on—"

Sharply, Lord Charlton said, "Just concentrate on drawing up the will, if you please, Ambrose, and drafting the advertisements."

Ambrose stood up. He said, "About the will, sir."

"What about it?"

"Well . . . supposing that we don't find Simon Warwick. Supposing he's dead, for instance."

8

"Then the money is to go to his eldest legitimate child. Nobody else. Not to the adoptive parents."

"I see. Eldest legitimate offspring—"

"So long as it's Simon's own child. I won't have any adopted brat taking over Warwick Industries."

Ambrose sighed again. "That may be tricky to draft," he said, "but I'll do my best. Now, supposing he's dead, leaving no children. Or supposing we just fail to trace him—"

"In that case, we shall have to revert to the old will, and those tiresome charities with which you deal so efficiently, Ambrose."

Ambrose's brain was ticking over fast. He said, "You see, sir, things that sound simple may have all sorts of legal complications."

"What do you mean?"

"We must consider many contingencies."

"Such as?"

"You know nothing about this young man, Lord Charlton. He might show no interest whatsoever in the business, and simply sell out and fritter the money away."

There was a moment of silence. Then Charlton said, "I don't believe that would happen. However, I take your point, Ambrose. I suppose we must attach some strings."

"Exactly, sir." Ambrose was relieved. "Shall we say that if we can trace Simon Warwick and prove his identity, he shall inherit provided that he takes his seat on the board of Warwick Industries and is active in the affairs of the company?"

"Very well. If you wish." Charlton sounded old and tired and bored.

"And if," Ambrose went on, "he should by disinclination or disability not concern himself in the business—"

"What do you mean by disability?" asked Lord Charlton sharply.

Ambrose said, a little desperately, "Well, sir, I'm just trying to cover everything. I mean—your nephew might be fatally ill or even legally insane. He might be in prison, or—oh, there are all sorts of situations which could prevent him from—"

Charlton held up his hand, and Ambrose fell silent. Then the old man said, "You are quite right, of course, Ambrose. I had a simple idea, and there is no such thing in law. Very well. Put in your insomuches and whereinafters and notwithstandings. Just make sure that if he is alive and legally competent and agreeable to the idea, my nephew shall inherit my interest in Warwick Industries. The same provisions to apply to the eldest legitimate child of his

9

body, on reaching the age of twenty-one. Otherwise, we go back to the old will."

"There's another thing, Lord Charlton," said Ambrose.

"Good God. Another? Are you lawyers never satisfied?"

"I'm only trying to protect your interests, Lord Charlton. Surely you see that you must set a time limit?"

"A time limit?"

"Yes. A clause stipulating that if Simon Warwick, or his eldest legitimate offspring, has not appeared to claim the inheritance within a certain period after your death—I would suggest a year—then the money goes to charity, as previously intended."

Lord Charlton considered. "A year is too short a time," he said at last. "Five years."

"I submit, sir, that five years is too long. If, after the most active and exhaustive inquiries, we have not located your nephew within a year—"

"Very well. Make it three years. No less."

"Could we not compromise with two, sir? The legal complications and the burden on the estate—"

"I said three years, Ambrose. You have three years after my death to find Simon Warwick. All expenses for the search will be paid from the estate, of course." He stopped, and frowned. "What am I doing, talking as though I were dead already? Get moving, Ambrose, my boy. I intend to meet my nephew Simon before I die."

Later that evening, by the fireside in Ealing, Rosalie Quince said to her husband, "Is there a hope in hell of finding him, Ambrose?"

"I don't know, darling. I doubt it. But I shall certainly have to try. The old man has made up his mind."

The following day, Ambrose drafted the new will and took it to Belgrave Terrace for Lord Charlton's signature. Later in the week, the advertisements appeared in the columns of the *Times*, *Telegraph*, *Guardian*, *Washington Post*, *The New York Times*, *Christian Science Monitor*, and other prominent British and American newspapers. A couple of days later, journalists began besieging Lord Charlton's place of business and his residence, smoking with questions. Ambrose deflected them as best he could, but in no time the rumor was running that the mysterious Simon Warwick was Lord Charlton's long-lost nephew and stood to inherit a fortune. As Ambrose remarked morosely to Rosalie, there was no need to advertise any more. Anybody, on either side of the Atlantic, who read a newspaper must know that Simon Warwick was requested to contact Messrs. Quince, Quince, Quince and Quince, where he would learn something to his advantage.

Three weeks later, Lord Charlton died, very peacefully. It was after dinner, and he was sitting in his favorite armchair in the library, with a glass of fine old brandy in one hand and a big cigar in the other. A smell of burning attracted the butler from the hall. He found his master dying, with the Georgian brandy bubble, miraculously unbroken, rolling on the floor beside him, its contents sinking into the crimson carpet. The cigar had burned a neat round hole in the leather upholstery of the chair.

The butler telephoned the doctor, and then returned to Lord Charlton, who murmured just three words. "Ambrose . . . Simon . . . I . . ." Then he died.

It was a week after Lord Charlton's death—on Christmas Eve, to be precise—that the first claimant turned up in Ambrose's office, asserting that without any possible doubt he was Simon Warwick.

2

The young man who faced Ambrose Quince across the desk in the Theobald's Road office looked exactly as Lord Charlton had predicted—the very epitome of a rising young American executive. He was clean shaven, blue eyed, and he wore his dark blond hair neatly trimmed. He was dressed in dark gray double-knit woolen pants, a navy-blue blazer, a spotless white shirt, and a club tie. When he smiled, he showed even white teeth, and he obviously used all the right deodorants and mouthwashes.

Ambrose regarded him with very little enthusiasm, uncomfortably aware of his own crumpled suit and the small egg stain on his tie. He said. "So you claim to be Simon Warwick, do you?"

The young man smiled. "I am Simon Warwick, Mr. Quince. I can prove it."

"I'm glad to hear that," said Ambrose dryly. "Do you have your passport with you?"

The smile deepened, attractively. "Certainly." The visitor reached into his breast pocket and pulled out a United States passport, which he handed to Ambrose.

The solicitor ruffled through the pages in silence, and then said, "This passport is made out to Harold R. Benson, Jr., born on October 28, 1944, in Leesburg, Virginia. I don't see any mention of Simon Warwick, Mr. Benson."

"Would you expect to, sir?"

12

Ambrose resented being called "sir" by a man of his own age. He said, "I am asking the questions, Mr. Benson. May I ask where you saw our advertisement?"

"Certainly you may. In the *Washington Post*. As a matter of fact, it was my wife who noticed it. She has more time to read the papers, now that Hank is away at school all day."

"Hank?"

"Our son. Harold R. Benson the Third. He's eight."

"And how did Mrs. Benson know that she was, in fact, married to Simon Warwick?" Ambrose used the tone of voice that he employed in court when trying to unsettle a witness.

He was rewarded with a smile so broad as to be almost a chuckle. "Mr. Quince, wouldn't it be easier if I just told you the story of my life—documented where necessary?"

"Very well." Ambrose sat back, put the tips of his fingers together, and tried to look inscrutable. In fact, he was trying to make up his mind about the personable Mr. Benson, and failing. "Let's have it, then. From the beginning."

Again the smile. "A pleasure, Mr. Quince. I was born here in London in 1944. My father was Dominic Warwick, younger brother of the late Lord Charlton. My mother was his wife, née the Honorable Mary Cheverton. I was only a week old when our house was hit by a flying bomb. Both my parents were killed. By some miracle, I survived. I was taken to Great Ormond Street Hospital for Children. Say, does that place still exist?"

"It does," said Ambrose.

"Then I shall pay it a visit and shake it by the hand."

"Get on with the story, please," said Ambrose.

"Well, my birth had been registered, although I was never christened." Like a conjurer producing a rabbit from a hat, Benson whisked a yellowing piece of paper out of his pocket and threw it on the desk. "Here's a copy of the birth certificate. Simon Alexander Warwick, born October 8, 1944."

"Not October 28, Mr. Benson?"

"Obviously not."

"How do you account for the discrepancy?"

"I'll come to that later."

"Where were you born?"

"What do you mean, Mr. Quince? I've told you. London."

Ambrose leaned forward. "At home, or in a hospital?"

Benson's brows drew together in a slight frown. "I don't know," he said. "She never told me."

13

"She?"

"My mother. That is, my adoptive mother. Maybe she didn't know herself. I've always imagined that it was at home."

"Home being where?"

"London, of course."

"The address?" Ambrose permitted himself a touch of sharpness.

Benson said, "Can't you read? It's there on the certificate. 23, Markham Mews, S.W. What I can't tell you for sure is whether I was born there or in a hospital."

"All right," said Ambrose. He felt he had been put in a one-down position. "Get on with it. What happened then?"

"What happened then was that my father and mother—the Bensons, I mean—were contacted by a lawyer, offering me for adoption."

"Name of the lawyer?"

"I'm sorry. I don't know."

Ambrose wrote on his pad, "Doesn't know name of lawyer." He said, "Where did this anonymous lawyer have his place of business, Mr. Benson?"

"I don't know that, either."

Ambrose made another note. Benson, apparently impatient, said, "Hell, Mr. Quince, I'm just telling you what my mother told me. I can't be expected to know any more, can I?"

"I suppose not. Who was your adoptive father?"

"Harold Raymond Benson, Captain, United States Army. Married, in England in 1943, Joan Margaret Wheatley. You'll find all the papers you need here."

Out came another envelope. Very slowly and deliberately, Ambrose Quince inspected the various certificates. Then he said, "I see that both your parents are dead."

"Unfortunately, yes."

"There is a birth certificate here. Harold Raymond Benson, Jr. Born October 28, 1944, Leesburg, Virginia. It doesn't tally, does it, Mr. Benson?"

Benson said, "My adoptive parents wanted me to have a completely fresh start in life. They regarded my true date of birth as the date when they first took possession of me—if that's the right expression. October 28. All three of us arrived in the United States on November 7, after a slightly scary voyage—or so I'm told. My parents went to my father's home in Leesburg, and registered my birth there. I don't know just how they managed it, but they did it.

My father's family was . . . well, quite influential. You see, they never wanted me or anybody else to know that I was not their son."

"Really?" said Ambrose. "Then how did you come to find out?"

"I was hoping you would ask me that."

"Well?"

"I found this." Producing his trump card, Harold Benson laid a faded British passport on the desk. It had been issued in London, on October 28, 1944, and was in the name of Simon Alexander Warwick, infant. Blue eyes, fair hair. A pudgy little baby face, surrounded by lace and knitting, gazed peacefully out from the two-by-two-inch photograph. Date of birth, October 8, 1944. Place of birth, London. Nationality, British.

Sharply, Ambrose said, "Where did you get this?"

"I told you, sir. I found it among my father's papers, after he died. The birth certificate was with it. It didn't mean anything to me, of course—that is, I didn't connect it with myself. I took it to my mother, and asked her who the hell this Simon Warwick was."

"And what did she say?"

"She was very upset. If she hadn't been . . . if she'd just said it was a friend's child, or something . . . I mightn't have given it another thought. But she hit the ceiling. Said Dad should have destroyed all the documents years ago, that it could only make trouble, and so forth. Well, naturally that got me interested—especially as this Simon Warwick was almost exactly the same age that I was."

"How old were you when this happened, Mr. Benson?"

"I was fifteen. A bad age. A bad age to lose one's father. A bad age for a kid to start suspecting that he may never have been that father's son. I'm not proud of what I did. My mom was upset enough at Dad's death—it was a heart attack, completely unexpected. I'm afraid I bullied her and shouted at her, and in the end she told me the truth. That I was adopted. That I had been born Simon Warwick, in London. That she knew she could never have children of her own, so she and Dad took me over when my real parents were killed in a raid on London. I made her tell me everything she knew about my real parents—which wasn't much apart from their names and their address. One thing I never could get out of her was the name of the attorney who had arranged the adoption. She said he was probably still alive, and she would only tell me about dead people, because she said they couldn't be hurt."

Ambrose said, "How did you react to all this?"

"At first I was pretty well broken up. It's . . . well, it's unsettling to find out you're not the person you thought you were. Kids worry about that sort of thing. But after a bit—well, I guess I just learned to live with it. Pretty soon afterward I went away to college in D.C.—George Washington University. My mother sold the old house and went to live in an apartment. I didn't see that much of her, I'm afraid. I wasn't even home when she died. I kept the documents, but I never told anybody who I really was—except my wife, when we got engaged. I reckoned she had the right to know whom she was marrying. That's how she came to spot the ad in the *Post*."

Ambrose considered for a moment. Then he said, "Your mother sold the house. So you don't still live in Leesburg, Virginia?"

"Oh, no. We're in Charlottesville now. Because of the university."

"I'm afraid, Mr. Benson," said Ambrose, "that my knowledge of American geography is limited. Would you explain?"

Benson smiled again. He said, "I should have thought that even . . . that is, the University of Virginia is not exactly unknown outside the States. Thomas Jefferson founded it in Charlottesville in 1819, after he retired—he lived nearby at Monticello. He designed most of the principal buildings himself. The Rotunda—"

"I just asked for an explanation, Mr. Benson, not a history lesson."

"Sorry, sir. Well, I teach at the university, you see. English literature is my subject. So of course we live in Charlottesville."

"I see. Now, you say you have known for some years that you were Simon Warwick. Did you also know that you were Lord Charlton's nephew?"

Benson flushed. "Of course not. I told you, my mother would only mention people who were dead when she told me about my real family. And since my uncle changed his name when he got his peerage, it never even occurred to me—until I saw the story in the papers."

Ambrose said, "The connection between the late Lord Charlton and Simon Warwick was only publicized some days after the original advertisement. I notice that you made no attempt to get in touch with me until you realized that a considerable amount was at stake."

Angrily, Benson said, "I know nothing about what's at stake. Only rumors. I came here as quickly as I could, after Sally spotted the ad. I couldn't leave the university until the Christmas vacation."

"You didn't think of writing to us?"

"No, I didn't. It would have been a waste of time. I obviously had to show you the documents, and I certainly wasn't about to send them through the mail."

For a moment, the two men looked at each other with unfriendly eyes. Then Quince said, "Well, of course, all this will have to be checked out, Mr. Benson. I'm sure you understand that."

"Of course, Mr. Quince."

"So if you'll just leave the documents with me—"

"I'll do no such thing, Mr. Quince." With a swift movement, Benson gathered up the papers and returned them to his pocket. "I have had photocopies made for you. Here." He opened his slim briefcase and took out an envelope. "You'll find everything there. The passport has been copied page by page, even though most of them are blank. You'll see the U.S. visa, the exit stamp from the United Kingdom on October 30, 1944, and the entry into the United States on November 7. It was a long trip. The convoy was attacked by U-boats and a couple of the merchant ships were damaged and slowed us all down. That's what my mother told me. You can probably check that out as well."

Ambrose decided not to make an issue of it. He inspected the contents of the envelope in silence, and then said, "Yes, everything seems to be here. This will do for our preliminary investigations. Where are you staying, Mr. Benson?"

"The Marlow Court Hotel in Kensington, sir."

Ambrose produced an icy smile. "We will be in touch, Mr. Benson."

"How long is all this going to take, Mr. Quince? I mean, the Christmas vacation ends on—"

Ambrose stood up. "I'm afraid, Mr. Benson, that we cannot hurry our investigation. However, it may not be necessary for you to stay in the country. We can always contact you in . . . er . . . Charlottetown."

"Charlottesville, Mr. Quince. But don't worry, I shall stay here. The university will give me leave of absence."

Ambrose inclined his head slightly. "As you wish, Mr. Benson. You will be hearing from us."

Rosalie Quince leaned forward and peered intently into the mirror as she applied dark brown mascara to her long lashes. She said, "What do you think, Ambrose? Can he possibly be genuine?"

Ambrose, struggling to make a perfect butterfly bow out of his

17

black tie, said, "I don't believe him. He's a fake."

"What makes you so sure, darling?"

"Because he's so damned plausible, that's why."

Rosalie laughed. "That's a paradoxical reason for not believing him, isn't it?"

"He's exactly the sort of man old Charlton *expected* to turn up," said Ambrose. He gave his tie a sharp tweak, and it came undone. "Damn this thing. Then there's the American birth certificate and the wrong date of birth. The whole story stinks."

Rosalie regarded her beautiful, pale reflected face, and made a moue. "I wish I didn't have to wear this awful old rag tonight. Prudence always has such marvelous clothes."

"You look lovely, darling," said Ambrose gallantly.

"Oh, don't be idiotic." Rosalie gave her shoulders a little, impatient shake, and arranged the slim straps of her dress. "What about the passport? How could he possibly have got the passport unless he was Simon Warwick? Doesn't that make it fairly conclusive?"

"Not if I can help it," Ambrose said. "Come and tie this bloody thing for me, will you, darling?"

"Okay." Rosalie's deft fingers flickered, and the black silk fell obediently into shape. "Did Michael say who else is going to be there tonight?"

"Just himself and Prudence and one other couple. People by the name of Tibbett. He's some sort of big noise at Scotland Yard. They're old friends of the Barkers'—you know how many police prosecutions Michael does."

Rosalie said, "Well, perhaps this Tibbett can help you explode your fake Simon Warwick. If he is a fake."

"And if he's not—"

"Come on, Ambrose. We're late already and it's a filthy night. Why does it always have to rain on Christmas Eve?"

Prudence and Michael Barker were celebrated for their small dinner parties, but they had had no intention of giving one on Christmas Eve. Their idea had been to share a quiet meal with their old friends, Chief Superintendent Henry Tibbett of Scotland Yard and his wife, Emmy. In fact, it had become something of a tradition over the past few years. Christmas is a time for family reunions, but the Tibbetts were childless and the three Barker girls were grown, married, and widely scattered over the world. So the Tibbetts and the Barkers had fallen into the pleasant habit of dining together on

Christmas Eve, and Prudence has issued the expected invitation in mid-December.

Michael Barker was surprised, therefore, to get a telephone call from Henry on December 21.

"Michael? Henry here. Look, old man—I wonder if I might ask a favor of you."

"A favor? Of course. What is it?"

"You know Ambrose Quince, don't you?"

"Yes. Not very well. His father and mine were friends. Is it about this Simon Warwick business? Nothing criminal there, I hope."

"No, no," said Henry. "It's just that . . . well, I'd like to meet him." He hesitated. "You . . . I hate to ask you this, Michael . . . you wouldn't invite them on Christmas Eve, would you?"

Michael was taken aback. "Well . . . I suppose we could . . . doubt if they'd be able to come at such short—"

Henry said, "I really can't explain, Michael. It's just that my . . . that these Simon Warwick advertisements have interested me. There's a great deal of money involved, you know, and also control of a very important group of companies."

"And a peerage?" said Michael.

"No—Charlton was a life peer. Fortunately. Otherwise, it would have been a situation of comic-opera complexity. Will you apologize to Prue and humor me, Michael? I'd really like to meet Quince, in a purely social situation."

"Oh, very well. I'll give him a call now. I suppose he'll have to consult with Rosalie and ring us back."

Later that evening, Prudence Barker answered the telephone.

"Oh, hello . . . yes . . . yes . . . yes, that's right . . . good . . . about seven-thirty . . . see you then . . ." She put down the receiver, and said to her husband, "The Quinces will be delighted to come on Wednesday."

"Well, I'm damned," said Michael Barker. "I never thought—"

"Almost certainly," said Prudence, "Rosalie will have had to cancel something else. But she would never refuse an invitation from you."

"It was from you."

"Don't be silly. It was from us, to dine at this house. You are a Queen's Counsel and therefore socially desirable. It's a pity, because I like Rosalie in many ways. I just wish she wasn't so blatantly ambitious. It makes me feel . . . exploited."

"I'm the one who should feel exploited," said Michael. "It was Henry who insisted we ask the wretched Quinces."

"Then," said Prudence, "Henry will have had a good reason. Let's make it a good party."

To everybody's surprise, it was a good party. Rosalie Quince, despite her old dress, looked exquisite and behaved beautifully. Emmy Tibbett, merry and dark haired and fighting a losing battle with plumpness, put everybody at their ease by her genuine pleasure in meeting new acquaintances. Henry, mild mannered and sandy haired, encouraged Ambrose Quince to expand his sense of importance. Prudence served simple, excellent food and Michael excellent and rather expensive wine. As coffee was served, the conversation inevitably turned to the topic of Simon Warwick.

Ambrose, mellow with wine, was prepared to regard this as a privileged occasion, and lowered his normally rigid defenses.

"Yes," he said, puffing on one of Michael's cigars. "Yes, it's an interesting situation. And—just between these four walls—our first client turned up today."

"Claiming to be Simon Warwick?" Henry asked.

"More than claiming. Insisting. With the whole story pat *and* the original Warwick baby's passport."

"Do you believe him?" Prudence asked.

"Frankly, Mrs. Barker—no, I don't. But it's going to be difficult to prove or disprove his claim, one way or the other."

Henry said, "Correct me if I'm wrong, Michael—but I should have thought that this would be a matter for a court to decide. I mean—Charlton's executors should surely challenge the authenticity of any claimant, however convincing, if only to throw the ball into the lap of the judiciary and force the court to make a ruling."

"Of course," said Michael. "That's what you are planning, isn't it, Quince?"

Before Ambrose could answer, Rosalie said, "It would be no easier for anybody to substantiate a claim in a court than out of it."

"No easier," said Henry, "but more binding in law, once the decision was given. If Mr. Quince were to decide on his own, as executor, to recognize a claimant—"

"I appreciate your good advice, Chief Superintendent," said Ambrose, with more than a touch of irony. "However, I am not proposing to recognize anybody at this stage. Apart from a few crank letters, we've only had this one fellow, and I think we shall be able to dispose of him without too much difficulty."

On December 29, when Messrs. Quince, Quince, Quince and Quince reopened for business after the Christmas holiday, the second claimant turned up.

Simon Finch could hardly have been more different from Harold R. Benson, Jr., if he had been studying for the part. He was a tall, gangling man, untidily put together, with hands and feet that seemed too large for his thin body. His face was long and creased, and his blue eyes were vague behind thick-lensed glasses. His gray pin-striped suit was considerably shabbier than Ambrose's, and his shirt looked as though it was nearing the end of a week of wear. His shoes were scuffed and his socks, although both blue, did not match. When he spoke, his voice was high pitched and nervous, with a middle-class English accent. Not at all the sort of man who Lord Charlton had hoped would take over the running of his empire.

"Mr. Quince?" he said. He threw back his head in a nervous gesture, causing his Adam's apple to wobble.

"I am Ambrose Quince, yes."

"I'm pleased to meet you, Mr. Quince. I am Simon Warwick."

Ambrose regarded his visitor with disbelief. Then he said, "My secretary announced Mr. Simon Finch."

"Well, yes, of course she did. I am Simon Finch. But I am also Simon Warwick. That is, I used to be Simon Warwick."

"How surprising. Can you prove it?"

"Oh yes. Certainly. Of course. I wouldn't be here otherwise, would I?"

"Very well," said Ambrose. "Go ahead. Prove it."

"I hardly know where to start, Mr. Quince. With my birth, I suppose. My real parents were Lord Charlton's brother, Dominic Warwick, and his wife, Mary. They were killed in London by a flying bomb when I was a small baby—only a week old, in fact. Neither family wanted me. I imagine that my mother's people had disapproved of her marriage, and that Alexander Warwick was too busy." Finch's thin mouth clamped shut in an expression at once disgusted and deeply hurt.

"Go on," said Ambrose.

"Fortunately for me, Alexander Warwick did business with a solicitor in Marstone—one Alfred Humberton. There was a big American military camp near Marstone, and Humberton knew of a certain Captain John Finch and his English wife, who wanted to adopt a baby before going back to the States. Captain Finch had been wounded and was being invalided home. So it was arranged. I traveled with the Finches to America on a British passport in the name of Simon Warwick, but once we got there, I became Simon Finch."

Ambrose had gone rather pale. He said, "How do you know all this?"

Finch creased his face into the semblance of a smile. He took an envelope out of his pocket and handed it to the lawyer. "These are photocopies, of course," he said. "I have the originals. They are the letters Humberton wrote to the Finches."

Ambrose extracted the sheets of stiff photocopy paper from the envelope, and unfolded them. There were three letters, on Humberton's headed notepaper. The first started, "Dear Captain Finch, I believe I may have found a baby suitable for immediate adoption . . ." The second was concerned with practical details, and included the sentence, "I have applied for a passport on his behalf . . ." The last read, "Dear Captain Finch, I am delighted that all is now arranged, and that you and Mrs. Finch will collect the little chap from my office at 2:30 p.m. next Tuesday. I note that you sail on Thursday, and wish you a safe and speedy voyage . . ." The correspondence appeared to have taken place during the last weeks of October 1944.

Ambrose said, "How did these documents come into your possession, Mr. Finch?"

"How? From my parents, of course."

"There is no mention of the name Simon Warwick, Mr. Finch. I suppose you know that Mr. Humberton arranged other private adoptions?"

"You think he arranged another adoption that same week, to another American army captain sailing for home with his English wife?"

Ambrose let this pass. He said, "How and when did you learn your true identity, Mr. Finch?"

Finch said, "When I was fifteen, I happened to find these papers, and realized I was adopted. I persuaded my mother to tell me my real name. She knew it, of course, even though as a matter of policy it was not written in the letters. It was . . . a traumatic experience, Mr. Quince. As a result, I ran away from home. My childhood had not been very happy, you see."

"It strikes me, Mr. Finch," said Ambrose, "that you appear to be completely English, rather than American."

"That's true. My adoptive mother was English, of course, and I

22

have lived in this country since I was fifteen. When I ran away, it was to England."

"You traveled on a United States passport?"

"Not my own." Finch paused. "Perhaps I had better explain."

"I think you should, Mr. Finch."

"Well, at the age of fifteen I visited this country with my parents, traveling with them on a joint family passport. I knew my true identity by then, and I was secretly determined to stay in England. I . . . acquired . . . the documents relating to my adoption before we left home. Once here, I persuaded my parents to enroll me at an English school and go home without me. I then ran away from school."

"And they never tried to find you?" Ambrose was incredulous.

"They may have done. They did not succeed. Frankly, I think they were as pleased to be rid of me as I was of them."

"And what about your position here? Are you a naturalized Englishman?"

"Why should I be? I was born here."

Ambrose said, impatiently, "You know what I mean. What passport do you hold? Where are your identity documents?"

Finch held up a thin hand. "All lawyers are alike. They think only in terms of documents. Ordinary people are simpler. I have no documents, Mr. Quince. I have never applied for a passport. I live my quiet bachelor life in Westbourne, and mind my own business. Should I ever need documents, I would produce the evidence I have shown you, with my birth certificate as Simon Warwick, which is filed at Somerset House. I call myself Simon Finch, because I have become accustomed to the name—but I am Simon Warwick and I have proved it."

"Your date of birth?"

"October 8, 1944. It's there in one of the letters."

"What happened to the passport issued to you as a baby?"

Finch shrugged. "I have no idea. I suppose the Finches destroyed it."

"Well," said Ambrose, "the matter can be cleared up quite simply. I will contact Captain and Mrs. Finch. Do you have their address?"

"I do not. We have not corresponded for nearly twenty years. The last address I know is the one mentioned in those letters, in McLean, Virginia. I have no idea whether they are still there—or indeed, if they are still alive."

"It's all very unsatisfactory, Mr. Finch," Ambrose said. "We

23

shall have to check it out very carefully."

"Of course you will, Mr. Quince. I suppose you are getting the usual collection of frauds, pretending to be me. But none of them has the documents that I have."

Ambrose stood up. "We have your Westbourne address, Mr. Finch. We will be in touch with you in due course."

3

Four days later, Ambrose and Rosalie Quince boarded a jet airliner at Heathrow Airport and flew to Washington, D.C. At a meeting with the other executor of Lord Charlton's will—a representative of his London bank—it had been decided that a personal investigation of the backgrounds of the two claimants was more than justified, since each seemed to possess an inexplicable amount of documentation. The cost of a first-class return ticket for Ambrose had been debited to the estate, but Ambrose had traded this for two economy-class fares, paid the difference out of his own pocket, and taken Rosalie along.

Winter had struck Washington with the capricious ferocity that it displays at five- or six-year intervals. The city was mantled in frozen snow, which had turned from white to dingy gray, and the streets were like skating rinks. A biting wind whipped in from the north, sending booted and furred pedestrians scurrying into doorways to shelter from the thin, vicious sleet that it drove before it. Narrow traffic lanes had been thawed out with sprinkled salt along the main thoroughfares, but the side streets remained slithery death-traps, and most of the local cars seemed to have been recently dented.

Ambrose and Rosalie stayed overnight at one of the city's pleasant, slightly shabby, turn-of-the-century hotels, and the next day ventured forth with some trepidation in a rented car, headed for Leesburg, Virginia. The combination of the icy roads and the unfamiliar automatic transmission proved tricky at first, but Ambrose was rightly proud of his dexterity as a driver, and soon they were making good progress through the snow-covered countryside of Virginia, past white-fenced farms and colonial mansions perched on hilltops, proud and upright behind the tall white columns that Thomas Jefferson had made fashionable two hundred years earlier.

Cherry Mount, Leesburg—the address that Harold R. Benson, Jr., had given Ambrose as his childhood home—turned out to be a smallish but exquisite example of such a mansion, several miles outside Leesburg and standing in about twenty acres of rolling grassland. Ambrose maneuvered the car with difficulty up the ice-rutted lane from the main road, noting with a pang of envy the stables, the large swimming pool tarpaulined for the winter, and the neat hedged garden around the house. Harold R. Benson, Jr., whoever he really was, had been reared in circumstances of considerable affluence.

The present owners of the house, who had been warned of Ambrose's visit, were U.S. Air Force Colonel Withers, currently employed at the Pentagon, and his very Southern wife. They were charming and hospitable, but could help very little when it came to the Bensons. They had bought Cherry Mount, they said, ten years earlier from the widowed Mrs. Benson, who had been living there on her own since the death of her husband and the departure of her son to George Washington University.

"Mrs. Benson was a very gracious lady," said Melanie Withers. "Y'all must understand that she felt deeply about this house. It had been in her husband's family for several generations, you see. Coming from England as she did, she had a great sense of tradition, and she did *not* want to leave her home. We appreciated that, but she told us her son had finally convinced her that this place was too big for just one little person. Such a nice, good-looking boy, wasn't he, Arthur? I understand he's a professor at the university now, and married with a boy of his own. How the time does go by! Anyways, Mrs. Benson agreed to sell the house, and she moved to an apartment in town. It can't have been more than a year later that we read about her death in the paper. Pneumonia, it said, but I always had the feeling that maybe she was just pining for this old house. Mrs. Benson was *not* the sort of lady to live in an apartment."

26

Rosalie looked up, caught her husband's eye, and quickly looked away again, afraid that she might disgrace herself by giggling. The colonel's lady, with true-blue Southern logic, was apparently suggesting that English-born Mrs. Benson had shown no more than well-bred delicacy in deciding to die rather than to live in an apartment.

Colonel Withers said, "Since you're interested in the Bensons, Mr. Quince, we took the liberty of inviting some people over for drinks—neighbors who knew them when they lived here. They should be able to tell you more than we can. I hope that the snow hasn't . . . ah, I think I hear a car now. That'll be Mark and Lucy." He hurried out to open the front door.

Mark and Lucy Pettigrew were a sprightly couple, both in their late sixties, and it soon transpired that they lived two miles away and were the Witherses' nearest neighbors. The Bensons had been living at Cherry Mount when the Pettigrews arrived in Leesburg, nearly thirty years ago. Little Harry must have been about five then. How exciting that he might stand to inherit some money from English relations. Of course, Joan Benson had been English— everybody knew that. Harold had met and married her when he was over there during the Second World War, and had brought her back to live in this house, which he had inherited from his father.

Ambrose asked if Captain Benson had been wounded in the war, but nobody seemed to know. If he had been, it was never mentioned. He had died most tragically of a heart attack, at an early age.

The conversation then turned to the weather, the difficulty of exercising the horses, and a certain amount of spicy local gossip and politics. As tactfully as he could, Ambrose detached Lucy Pettigrew from the others, and asked her if she had known that Harry Benson, Jr., was an adopted child.

Lucy opened her black-rimmed eyes wide. "Adopted? You have to be joking, Mr. Quince. Did you hear that, Mark? Mr. Quince says young Harry Benson may have been adopted! Well, of course, there's no proving it one way or the other, and it's true the Bensons didn't have any other children . . . but it seems an extraordinary idea. They were such a close-knit family, weren't they, Mark? Oh, I wouldn't believe *that* story, Mr. Quince, especially if it might stand in the way of a legacy for Harry. Thank you, Melanie, another martini would be just dandy."

Back at the hotel in Washington, Ambrose said to Rosalie, "The whole thing stinks. It's ridiculous. If what Benson says is true, his

27

parents were still in England on October 28, 1944, and yet a birth certificate was issued alleging that Harold Raymond Benson, Jr., was born at Cherry Mount, Leesburg, on that day."

Rosalie said, "This is the South, Ambrose. Families like the Bensons obviously had great influence and power—and still have, I believe. Maybe they simply turned up in November and gave a set of facts to the registrar, and looked him straight in the eye—and he issued the certificate. What puzzles me more is—why?"

"What do you mean—why?"

"I mean, I feel it's easier to believe that the Bensons fixed the birth certificate than that somebody like Harold Benson should come forward with this story if it's not true. He's obviously not an adventurer. He's a university teacher, comfortably off and with an impeccable family background. Why should he do it?"

Ambrose sighed. "I've long ago given up trying to pinpoint people's motives, darling," he said. "Any lawyer knows that even apparent pillars of society can and do behave quite irrationally at times." He paused. "Anyhow, there's nothing particularly eccentric about wanting to lay hands on a couple of million pounds. University teaching isn't the highest paid of professions."

"He has Simon Warwick's passport," Rosalie pointed out.

"That's obviously the clue to the whole business," said Ambrose. "He somehow came by the passport, and that gave him the idea of coming to England and passing himself off as Simon Warwick. If we could just find out where he got it . . . Ah, well, perhaps we'll get somewhere when we see his wife tomorrow."

"You spoke to her on the telephone, didn't you? What does she sound like?"

"A nice woman, by her voice. Not a Southern accent, like those two comic turns this afternoon. Soft spoken, northeast seaboard, I'd say. Not so very different from English, really."

Rosalie said, "She doesn't sound like the sort of woman who'd go along with this sort of deception."

"Maybe she's deceived, too. Maybe he's convinced her that he really is Simon Warwick. He might well have convinced us, remember, if we hadn't such strong reason to believe that the name of the adoptive parents was Finch."

"Hm." Rosalie sounded doubtful. "I'm not believing anything for the moment. I'm just looking forward to seeing Charlottesville. I hope the snow lets up."

The Quinces were lucky. The next day, the sun shone from a

chilly blue sky and sparkled on the Virginia countryside as they drove southwest from Washington toward the impressive skyline of the Blue Ridge Mountains. It was Friday, and already people in cars carrying skis were bowling along the salted, snow-free highway toward Warrenton and Culpeper, heading for a weekend at one of Virginia's ski resorts. In less than three hours, when the flat-topped mountain range was towering close ahead, the Quinces came to the university town of Charlottesville.

In many ways, Charlottesville is the University of Virginia, and the University of Virginia is Thomas Jefferson. In his old age, after his political career was over, long after the design and building of his own beautiful house, Jefferson turned his multi-skilled mind to his last project—the creation of a great university for his home state.

A Renaissance man strayed into the eighteenth century, Jefferson was diplomat and statesman, traveler, inventor, politician, architect, writer, and artist. For his home, Monticello, he personally designed every detail, down to the drapes: he invented and installed, among other things, self-opening doors, a seven-day clock run by huge pulleys and weights, a lift for sending dishes up to the dining room from the kitchen, so that confidential political dinner conversation could be carried on without the presence of servants, and a duplicating machine enabling two longhand copies to be written simultaneously. His European travels as American ambassador to France shaped his taste to an exquisite expression of neo-classicism. Clean, clear lines and elegant geometrical conceptions characterize his architectural designs—octagons and spirals, circles set in squares, and ovals set in circles.

The main buildings of the university represent his crowning achievement. Two great colonnaded buildings, of rose-red brick and white stucco, face each other across a sweep of green lawn; and at one end, linked by colonnades to the side-buildings and—in Jefferson's original conception—gazing out down the greensward to the distant mountains, stands the great Rotunda; that domed circle in a square, with oval rooms nestled like eggs within the circle, and all the orders of classical architecture meticulously reproduced for the edification of the students. It was little wonder that Queen Elizabeth II of England, on her trip to the United States during the bicentennial, picked this building as the one place of her own choice to visit.

When Ambrose and Rosalie arrived, the great lawn was a carpet

29

of unbroken white, and the bare trees were outlined in rime. Several visitors were busily clicking away with cameras, posing family groups on the Rotunda steps and admonishing their children not to throw snowballs; but the place had the unfulfilled air of a college on vacation, a sense of the buildings catnapping, breathing lightly, waiting for the bustle of life to return.

The address that Harold Benson had given Ambrose turned out to be one of the apartments under the colonnade—quarters that Jefferson had envisaged as housing undergraduates, but now the privileged dwellings of university staff. Rosalie rang the bell, and the door was opened almost at once by a smiling black girl wearing a dark dress and a neat white apron.

"Mr. and Mrs. Quince?" she said.

"That's right," said Ambrose. "Mrs. Benson is expecting us."

"I'm real sorry," said the girl. "Miz Benson's not here right now. Won't you come in? She left a note for you."

Ambrose and Rosalie exchanged a quick glance. Rosalie said, "When will she be back? We've driven all the way from Washington on purpose to—"

"If you'll just come in the drawing room. She left you a note."

Ambrose and Rosalie were ushered into a cheerful and beautifully proportioned room, furnished with antiques and chintz and smelling of lavender and wax polish. A log fire crackled in the grate, and propped on the mantelpiece above it was an envelope, addressed in a firm, forward-sloping hand to Mr. and Mrs. Ambrose Quince.

Ambrose tore open the envelope and read aloud. "Dear Mr. and Mrs. Quince, I am most sincerely sorry that I cannot meet you today. I tried to telephone your Washington hotel, but you had already left, so all I can do is ask Bettina to make sure you get this note. The fact is that I received a call this morning telling me that my son has been taken ill. He is up at a ski camp in the mountains with a group of young friends. Nobody seems to know exactly what the trouble is, and the local doctor thought I should drive up to be with him. I'm afraid I have no idea how long I shall be away. If you will telephone me before you leave Washington, maybe we can set up another meeting, if I am here. Please forgive me. Sincerely, Sally Benson." Ambrose turned to his wife. "What a damned nuisance," he said.

"Coincidence, do you think?"

"How do I know? Convenient coincidence or a diplomatic cold

in the head. Well, she needn't think I'm leaving the States without seeing her—she's only putting off the evil hour, that's all. Where did that girl go?"

Ambrose went out into the paneled hallway. Through a half-open door, he saw the black girl energetically sweeping a carpet. He opened the door and went into what could only be Benson's study—a small, pleasant room, book-lined, the desk clear of papers in the absence of its owner. All that was on it was a large color photograph of an attractive, strong-featured girl—presumably the elusive Mrs. Benson.

The black girl suspended her sweeping and looked at Ambrose in mild inquiry. He said, "This camp in the mountains where Mrs. Benson's son is."

"Yes, sir?"

"Where is it? Is it far from here?"

"I don't know, sir. I surely don't know where Master Hank is."

"Did Mrs. Benson tell you when she'd be coming back?"

"No, sir. She told me Master Hank's not well, and she go off in the car. She say maybe two-three days. That's all I know."

"It's very annoying," said Ambrose grumpily. There was a pause. The maid resumed her sweeping.

Ambrose went back into the hall as Rosalie came out of the drawing room. "Well, that seems to be that. Nobody knows where she is, or how long for."

"Never mind, darling," said Rosalie. "Let's go and visit the Rotunda, get ourselves some lunch, and then go back to Washington."

The maid had come out of the study and transferred her attentions to an oriental rug in the hall. Rosalie said, "Bettina, can you tell us a good restaurant around here?"

The girl considered. Then she said, "Miz Benson go Boar's Head sometime."

"Where's that?"

"Couple miles out of town, toward the mountains."

"Thank you," said Rosalie. "We'll try it. Please ask Mrs. Benson to call us in Washington as soon as she gets back."

"Okay." The girl opened the front door. "Have a good day now."

The Boar's Head turned out to be a rambling hotel whose central building had once been a mill house. It was the centerpiece of a carefully landscaped estate of opulent houses. In the big, dark-paneled dining room, girls and men in eighteenth-century

31

costumes—mobcaps and velvet knee-breeches—served excellent food with smiling Southern hospitality.

As Ambrose and Rosalie were finishing their fried chicken, the maitre d'—a young man in modern dress—came to their table to inquire if they were enjoying their meal. They reassured him on that point, and Rosalie added, "We were very lucky to be directed here, being strangers from England. It was Mrs. Benson who recommended you."

The young man looked puzzled. "Mrs. Harold Benson, Jr.?"

"That's right. From the university."

"But you've just missed her."

Ambrose said, "What do you mean?"

"Why, Mrs. Benson finished lunch not half an hour ago. She was sitting at that table over there, on her own. Her husband's in England, as I expect you know. We had quite a chat. She told me she was lunching early, as she was spending the weekend with friends in Williamsburg, and she wanted to get there in daylight, in case the weather closes in. Why, you only missed her by about ten minutes."

"She didn't say anything about her son being ill?" Rosalie asked.

"Hank? No, not a word. I thought he was up at ski camp. Is something wrong?"

Ambrose said quickly, "No, no. Nothing's wrong. I'm sorry we missed Mrs. Benson."

The maitre d' smiled and moved to another table. Rosalie said, "*Well!*"

"That clinches it," said Ambrose grimly. "She knows her husband's an impostor, and she's afraid she might give the game away. Well, she's just made a big mistake. She would have done better to try to bluff it out."

"It's going to be very awkward when we do meet her," Rosalie said.

"You leave her to me," said Ambrose, with a sort of satisfaction. "She's told us exactly what we came here to find out, and the important thing now is that she should go on thinking she's fooled us. Once she suspects that we know the truth, she'll alert Benson and he'll simply disappear. No, thank you very much. I intend to nail that young man for fraud and impersonation and everything else in the book. He thinks he's too damn clever. Well, let him go on thinking it for a little longer. He'll find out soon enough who's clever."

Rosalie gave her husband a long, amused look. "Ambrose Quince is clever," she said.

Ambrose flushed. "I didn't exactly mean that," he said. "But at least I'm not stupid enough to be taken in by Harold Benson, Jr. D'you want a dessert?" he added, as a mobcapped waitress appeared with a large menu. "No? Neither do I. Just two coffees, please. Then back to Washington. Tomorrow, we'll start on Mr. Simon Finch."

4

Harold R. Benson, Jr., had at least provided Ambrose Quince with an ancestral mansion, an up-to-date address, and a live—if elusive—wife to visit. Simon Finch was a more difficult proposition. All that Ambrose had to go on was an address in suburban Washington dating back more than fifteen years. With the rapidly growing suburbs and the quick turnover of inhabitants that is even more marked in Washington, D.C., than in most American cities, Ambrose felt that his task was going to be far from easy.

The next day, Saturday, under a leaden sky that threatened more snow, Ambrose and Rosalie drove over Key Bridge from Georgetown to the Virginia bank of the Potomac River, and were soon in the expensive suburb of McLean. Everywhere, new houses were going up—large houses with colonial-type façades, big gardens, and swimming pools. The vast shopping center at Tyson's Corner enticed shoppers into the luxurious emporia of Bloomingdale's and Saks Fifth Avenue. Every house had at least two cars, many three or four.

Ambrose had some difficulty in tracing the address that Finch had given him. Old Colonial Drive turned out to be a country road that was rapidly assuming the appearance of a wealthy housing estate as new buildings went up. However, number 186—to Ambrose's relief—was still there. It was a pretty little stone house, smaller but much more solidly constructed than its newer neighbors.

The front door was answered by a dark-haired maid, who greeted the Quinces in Spanish. When Ambrose asked in English to speak to the lady of the house, the maid giggled, went red in the face, and fled—leaving Ambrose and Rosalie shivering on the doorstep. They heard a hurried consultation of female voices in Spanish, and then a tall, good-looking woman appeared from the back of the house.

In reasonable English, but with a heavy accent, she said, "May I 'elp you? I am afraid Maria speak no English."

Ambrose said, "I'm sorry to trouble you, madam. I'm trying to trace some people who used to live in this house. People by the name of Finch."

"Feench?" The woman frowned. "I know nobody of zat name. No Feench. My 'usband rent zis 'ouse. We are at the embassy just one year already. Before us was Señor Oliviera, Brazil embassy. No Feench."

The woman smiled, gave a little nod as if to indicate that the conversation was now at an end, and began to close the front door. A little desperately, Ambrose said, "Just a moment, please. Can't you—?" He searched his mind for inspiration, and it came. "Can't you give me the name of the owner of the house?"

"I . . . no, I don't zink I do zat." The woman hesitated. "You can ask ze agent. Ze real-estate agent."

"What's his name?" Ambrose asked eagerly.

"Bernard Grady and Company. Ask for Mrs. Mallison. I cannot 'elp you any more." The door closed quickly and firmly.

From the warmth and comfort of the shopping center, Ambrose telephoned Bernard Grady and Company, whose address was listed in the directory as being in the old town of Alexandria, further down the river.

A brisk female voice informed Ambrose that Mrs. Mallison was not in the office. She worked largely from her home, but in any case today she was at an open house.

"An open house?" Ambrose was puzzled. "A party, you mean?"

"An open house," the girl repeated.

"I'm sorry, I don't quite understand . . ."

"It's Saturday," the girl explained patiently. "The house is open. Mrs. Mallison is showing it. She'll be there all day."

Enlightenment dawned. "Oh, I see. Sorry to have been so

dense. We do things rather differently in England. You mean, anybody can walk in and view the house?"

"Of course."

"Can you give me the address?"

"Certainly." The voice, which had been showing signs of irritation, now became cordial. "It's in McLean." She gave Ambrose an address and concise directions. "Then take the next turn right off Dolley Madison Boulevard, and follow our signs to the house."

The house that Mrs. Mallison was showing turned out to be typical of an affluent suburb. It was probably not more than two or three years old, and it was a smaller and flimsier imitation of the Leesburg mansion that had been the Benson family home. The red-brick façade was only a thin veneer, the columns looked impressive but supported nothing. However, the general effect was attractive, and despite the enormous price tag and the inclement weather, quite a lot of Washington's house-hungry citizens had come to see it. There was an assortment of cars in the drive, and several couples—mostly in young middle age and all clearly prosperous—smiled politely to each other as they passed coming and going through the open front door.

Just inside the door, in the large hallway, a distinguished-looking woman with gray hair sat at a small desk, directing the visitors and answering their questions.

"Mrs. Mallison?" Ambrose inquired.

"Yes, indeed. Have you looked around the house yet?"

"As a matter of fact, no." Ambrose was somewhat surprised to observe that Mrs. Mallison appeared to be in sole charge of the operation. He had not yet realized that in the United States, unlike England, the business of real estate was almost entirely in the hands of such capable ladies.

"Well, do take a look, and then ask me anything you want to know." She smiled, and turned to respond to an inquiry about property taxes from an earnest young man in a turtleneck sweater.

Ambrose hesitated. Mrs. Mallison was clearly extremely busy, and he knew that he and Rosalie must look like any other couple who had come to view the house. It was not going to be easy to detach her from her work to talk about Captain and Mrs. Finch.

At that moment, an elderly man came in through the front door and stood surveying the scene with a pleased smile. He was stout and tall, and with his rosy cheeks and white hair and beard, he could have stepped into the role of Santa Claus with no makeup.

His appearance was in sharp contrast to that of the youngish couples around him, and he gave the impression of being both a larger-than-life character and a man of authority.

Mrs. Mallison looked up from her papers, smiled, and said, "Why, Mr. Grady. How kind of you to look in."

"Now, Anna, my dear," boomed Santa Claus, "just you carry on. Pay no attention to me. I just dropped by because this house is so close to home."

Ambrose hurried over. "You are Mr. Bernard Grady?"

"I certainly am, sir. This is a delightful home, is it not? One of the best that has come our way for some time. I can tell you're interested—but you'll have to talk to Anna about it. She's in sole charge of this property."

"As a matter of fact," Ambrose said, "it's not this house I'm concerned with. It's 186 Old Colonial Drive."

The white eyebrows went up. "My dear sir, I fear you have been misinformed. That house is not on the market."

"I know it isn't, Mr. Grady. Please let me explain. I am trying to trace some previous owners—people named Finch. I thought that I might be able to do so through the present owners—or even that the Finches might still own the house, and be renting it out. I called there, and the tenant referred me to your office."

Grady was looking thoughtful. He said, "What is your concern with the Finches, Mr. . . . . er . . . ?"

"Quince. Ambrose Quince. And this is my wife Rosalie. We're from England."

"I had guessed as much, sir," said Grady, with a twinkle. "Well, now, Mr. Quince—as I say, what is your concern?"

Ambrose felt a quickening of excitement. This old man obviously knew something. He said, "I wonder if we could go somewhere a little more private, Mr. Grady, and I'll explain."

Grady looked at him through bright blue eyes for a moment, and then said, "Let us go to my house. It is only just down the road. I have lived in McLean for many years. You have a car? Wonderful. Perhaps you will be kind enough to give me a ride. I came on foot."

Bernard Grady's house, like the Finch home, was clearly a relic of the days when McLean was a country village rather than a suburb. It was a solid red-brick house, standing behind a solid red-brick wall, and surrounded by a well-tended garden. Even through the snow, Ambrose could see the neat outlines of the flower beds.

Grady ushered the Quinces into a pleasant but rather impersonal drawing room, poured drinks, and then said, "If you have come all the way from England, I suppose it must be about the boy."

"The boy?"

"Young Simon Finch. I hope he's not in trouble."

Ambrose exhaled a deep breath. He said, "Quite the reverse. He may stand to come into some money." He paused. "So the Finches do still own the house?"

Grady shook his white head. "No, no, no. Unfortunately, they are both dead now. But for many years they were friends and neighbors of mine. Alice put the house in my hands after Jack died, ten years ago. She was English—but of course you knew that." Ambrose nodded. Grady went on: "I had no difficulty in selling the house for her at a good price. The trek to the suburbs was in full swing, and McLean was becoming fashionable. Alice moved into a small apartment in Alexandria. We . . . I saw quite a lot of her. My wife had died recently, you see, so we were able to sympathize with each other." He paused, remembering. "Yes, she was a charming woman. Never lost that Englishness, in all the years she lived here. Who knows, if things had been different, we might have . . . but there it was."

"You say she is dead, too," Ambrose said.

"Yes. Most tragically. Poor Alice. She was on her way home from a vacation in England. The plane crashed. She was not among the survivors."

It was Rosalie who said, "Was it a vacation, Mr. Grady? Or was she looking for Simon?"

Grady shook his head. "I don't know. I just don't know. She would never speak about him . . . that is, she used to talk to me about him as he had been when he was a little boy. But after he ran away—never. Naturally, I did not press her. It was a very sensitive subject."

Ambrose said, "Just how much do you know of what happened, Mr. Grady?"

"How much about what, Mr. Quince?"

"About the Finches. Their past history. When did you first meet them?"

Grady said, "The Finches were married in England during the war. About 1943, it must have been. In '44, Jack was badly wounded—lost his right leg below the knee. He was invalided home, and they arrived in the States when Simon was only a few weeks old. When Jack got well enough, he took some sort of

38

government job in Washington. I'm not sure what—he didn't mention his work much. Anyhow, they bought the house on Old Colonial Drive, and settled in there with the new baby."

Ambrose said, "Mr. Grady, did you know that Simon was not their child? That he was adopted?"

Grady shook his head, but without surprise. "I didn't know," he said, "but I suppose I might have guessed. That was probably the root of the trouble."

"What was the trouble, Mr. Grady?" Rosalie asked.

"I really don't know."

"But if you were a near neighbor for all those years—"

"No, no, Mrs. Quince. I'm afraid I have not made myself clear. One eighty-six Old Colonial Drive was *my* house. I sold it to Alice and Jack in 1944, when I was finally able to convince Uncle Sam that a man in his forties was not too old to make some active contribution to the war. I was sent overseas in an administrative capacity, and my wife went to live with her parents in North Carolina. I met the Finches only a couple of times over the sale of the house. I was greatly taken with them, I must say, and the baby was a fine little fellow."

"So when did you meet them again?" Ambrose asked.

Grady said, "When the war ended, I went and joined my wife in North Carolina. I had always worked in real estate—but I came back to find the firm I had worked for closed. There was no job for me. My father-in-law came to the rescue—took me into his family business. It was fifteen years before I had saved up enough to achieve my ambition—to come back to the Washington area and open my own real-estate business. My wife and I bought this house, and were delighted to find that the Finches were still living in our old home. Delighted—except for one thing. The boy, Simon, had run away from home. It happened just before we moved back here to McLean.

"It was a shattering blow to Jack and Alice. Especially to Alice, I think. It made Jack very angry. I gathered he'd been mighty critical of his son at times. Jack was a big tough guy, had been a great one for sports and so on, but with his bad leg he'd had to give it all up. Naturally, he hoped his son would grow up to do all the things he'd wanted to do himself—but it seems Simon wasn't that sort of boy at all. Diffident and studious was how Alice described him."

Ambrose thought of the thin, nervous man he had met in London, and nodded. He said, "So what exactly happened?"

"I can't tell you, Mr. Quince. Neither of them would talk about it. Jack simply flew into a rage if the boy's name was mentioned. He disowned him—said he wouldn't let him into the house if he did try to come back. Alice always said it was all bluster to hide how hurt and disappointed he really was. I don't know. At all events, Simon never did come home, as far as I know. However, if—as you suggested—Alice had had an inkling that the boy might be in England, it's perfectly possible that she might have gone over to look for him after Jack died. He'd never have allowed her to do such a thing while he was alive, of course."

Ambrose said, "She never told you where she thought he might be?"

The old man shook his head. "She never spoke of him. That is, she only spoke about his childhood, before it happened."

"And you never saw Simon Finch yourself, except as a tiny baby?"

"Never. Alice did show me a couple of snapshots, taken when he was about thirteen. She had managed to keep them hidden when Jack insisted on destroying all traces of his son, after he ran away."

Ambrose reached into his pocket and brought out a small, unflattering picture that he had insisted be taken in London of the man who claimed to be Simon Finch.

"Could that be him, Mr. Grady?"

Grady took the photograph, fumbled with his spectacle case, and set a pair of horn-rimmed glasses on his broad nose. He studied the picture in silence, then said, "It could be. It could be, Mr. Quince. But I can't go further than that. You're asking me to search my recollection of a photograph of a thirteen-year-old boy, and to tell you whether it's the same person as a photograph of a man in his thirties. My impression is that the lad's hair looked rather lighter in the snapshots than this man's—but that could be a trick of the light. Anyhow, fair hair tends to darken in middle age. Well, there it is. All I can say is—that man could be Simon Finch." He cleared his throat, handed back the photograph, and said, "I've told you all I know, Mr. Quince. Will you now relieve my curiosity with a few more details?"

Ambrose said, "Certainly, Mr. Grady. I told you that the baby was adopted. His parents were both killed in an air raid, and the rest of the family didn't want to know. However, belatedly, the child's bachelor uncle developed a conscience, and decided to leave his money to his nephew, if the latter could be found. The uncle is now dead. I am the executor of the will, and I am looking for Simon Finch."

"So you knew he had disappeared as a youngster?"

Ambrose evaded the question. He said, "I am in touch with the young man in this photograph. He may be Simon Finch."

"And is there a lot of money involved?"

Ambrose hesitated just too long. Up went the white eyebrows again, and Bernard Grady said, "Why, bless my soul, Mr. Quince. Are you trying to tell me that Simon Finch was born Simon Warwick?"

Rosalie laughed. "No, Mr. Grady. Ambrose has been trying *not* to tell you, but he's obviously failed."

"Why, I was reading a piece in the *Post* only the other day. The uncle was a duke or something. Millions of dollars at stake, it said. Well, I'll be gosh-darned." He sighed. "Poor Alice. She could have told me for sure. I'm afraid I haven't been much help."

"You've helped me a great deal, Mr. Grady," said Ambrose. "There's just one other thing. When the baby left England, he had a passport of his own. A British passport. Mrs. Finch never mentioned such a thing to you, did she?"

"Nope. Not that I can . . .. Hey, wait a minute. I've just remembered something."

"Yes?"

"It was when she showed me those pictures of Simon. She was just a little bitter against Jack. The only time I heard her criticize him. She said something like, 'These are all I have to remind me I ever had a son, Bernie. A couple of wretched little snapshots. Jack destroyed everything else. I can't even find his passport.' I said, 'Passport? You mean young Simon had a passport?'—and she seemed quite embarrassed. 'Oh,' she said, 'we got him one when we thought we might go abroad'—and then she changed the subject. I'd quite forgotten. But I remember it now, because it was the only time I ever thought that maybe Alice wasn't squaring with me. She was the most honest person, Mr. Quince."

Ambrose smiled. "Your instinct was right, Mr. Grady. The Finches did travel abroad with Simon, but he went on their joint passport, as their child. She must have been referring to his infant passport—and of course she couldn't explain to you without giving away the secret that he was adopted. She said she couldn't find it?"

"That's my recollection, Mr. Quince. It was nine years ago."

"Very interesting, Mr. Grady. Very interesting."

Bernard Grady performed a final service by directing Ambrose and Rosalie to the local records office. There, the following Monday, they discovered death certificates for John Turnbull

Finch and, dated a year later, Alice Mabel Finch. His cause of death was given as cardiac arrest, and hers as multiple injuries sustained in an aviation accident. There was no birth certificate for Simon Finch, of course, because he had been born outside the United States.

However, the local public-school records showed that Simon Alexander Finch, of 186 Old Colonial Drive, had attended the school for ten years, entering first grade at the age of five in 1949 and leaving "to continue his studies elsewhere" at the age of fifteen, having completed the tenth grade—an average but not brilliant pupil. Unfortunately, no teachers who had known young Finch were still at the school—but, as Ambrose remarked to Rosalie, everything tied in.

As they walked down the snowy street from the school, Ambrose said, "There ought to be another piece of paper somewhere."

"What do you mean, darling?"

"Well, I've been boning up on the question of adoptions, especially in the United States. Normally, of course, the adopted child is born American, like the adoptive parents. Once the adoption is finally legalized—and that can take some time, because there's a lot of careful checking done—then the parents are handed a new birth certificate for the child. It gives the place and date of birth correctly, but with the adoptive instead of the natural parents entered as mother and father."

"So," said Rosalie, "if they decide not to tell the child he's adopted, there's no way he could find out."

"Exactly. The actual records of the transaction are sealed away in some lawyer's office, and until very recently *nobody* could have access to them—not even the child himself when he grew up. I believe there's a new and less rigid law now, but it wouldn't have applied to this case. Anyhow, we have no idea what lawyer the Finches used. There's no hope of getting hold of any documents relating to an American adoption."

Tentatively, Rosalie said, "Wouldn't Humberton have . . . ?"

"We've seen the letters from Humberton," Ambrose said. "But the actual adoption must have been done over here."

"So what about the birth certificate?"

"Exactly. Now, if Simon had actually been the Finches' child, born in England while his father was on active service, he'd have had a British birth certificate, a British passport if he wanted one, and the option of dual nationality or of deciding one way or the other when he came of age. But there was no way the Finches could get a British birth certificate for Simon in their name. As we know, it's still on the British files in the name of Warwick."

"They must have realized the problem," said Rosalie.

"Certainly they must. They must have put it to the lawyer who acted for them here. And I'm just asking myself—if I had been that lawyer, what would I have advised?"

Rosalie said thoughtfully, "If he'd been their natural child—"

"That's it!" interrupted Ambrose, triumphantly.

"What's it?"

"Naturalization. In the most literal sense of the word. I'll bet it could be arranged, and I bet they did it, and there must be a record of it somewhere!"

There was. Simon Alexander Finch, son of Alice (née Bartlett) and Captain John Finch, born to them in London, England, on October 8, 1944, had been naturalized as a United States citizen in 1945. His mother had taken American nationality upon her marriage, as she was entitled to do, and in the circumstances the statutory fourteen years' residency clause had been suspended in the case of the child. Simon Alexander Warwick, Englishman, had become Simon Alexander Finch, U.S. citizen.

"There you are!" Ambrose said to Rosalie, as they sat in their hotel room looking out over the lights of Washington and listening to cars skidding into each other on the frozen streets. "Everything tallies, and it works on the psychological level, too."

"How do you mean, darling?"

"Well, the machismo father who sounds a frightful brute, with his gimpy leg, trying to lead a vicarious life of brawn and brawls through his son. The gentle English mother, trying to mediate between them. The boy must have been unhappy enough by the time he found those papers, which told him for the first time that these people were not his parents at all. It's no wonder he stole the documents and ran away. The father then flies into a rage and destroys all other papers and photographs, except the snapshots, which the mother manages to hide." Ambrose, warming to his theme, had dropped into the historical present—a device he liked to use in court. "But his mother does not tell Grady that the passport was destroyed—only that she cannot find it. What happened to it? Nobody exactly knows, but I intend to find out. Somehow or other, it falls into the hands of the boy Harold Benson. After all, Leesburg is not so far from McLean. The boys are the same age, and from the same social background. Maybe they go to summer camp together. Perhaps Simon Finch discovers his

43

passport before he finds the letters, and takes it to show to his friend."

Interrupting the flow, Rosalie said, "You're quite certain aren't you, Ambrose?"

"Certain about what?"

"That Simon Finch is Simon Warwick."

"I don't see how there can be any doubt about it. I've enough proof for any court of law. What I intend to do now is to find out just how Benson got that passport, and to expose him for what he is—a fraud, and an impostor."

"And Simon Finch will get Lord Charlton's money?"

"I shall lay the matter before the judiciary," said Ambrose.

"You do sound pompous, darling."

"Sorry, darling. What I mean is, I'll consult with Bertie Hamstone, and if he agrees we'll go to the courts and present the evidence. After that, the will can be proved and the estate handed over."

"And Simon Finch-Warwick will take over one of the biggest textile businesses in Europe."

"He won't take over, idiot. He'll be the major shareholder."

Rosalie yawned, stretching her arms above her head. Then she got up and walked over to the window. "I can't help feeling sorry for them, Ambrose."

"For whom?"

"All those lovely charities who would have got the money. I bet they were counting on it."

"Well, they'll have to look elsewhere," said Ambrose, "because we've found Simon Warwick."

Rosalie turned, smiled, and held out her arms. "How clever you are, darling. He's sure to be grateful, isn't he?"

Ambrose embraced his wife. "He bloody well ought to be," he said.

The question of a second visit to Charlottesville was never even mentioned. The Quinces flew back to London with the documentary evidence of naturalization, a statement by Bernard Grady, school attendance records, and death certificates. The search for Simon Warwick was over.

5

A few days after they got back to England, Ambrose and Rosalie Quince gave a small dinner party. The food and drink were excellent—Rosalie employed a professional caterer to do the food, and hired help in the kitchen for the dishes and serving—but nevertheless the atmosphere was not exactly festive, nor was the occasion purely social. The guest list consisted of Sir Percy and Lady Diana Crumble, Mr. and Mrs. Bertram Hamstone, Miss Cecily Smeed, and Mr. Denton Westbury.

After dinner, when the hired help had removed the last dirty dish and had served coffee and liqueurs at the dinner table, Ambrose brought the meeting to order.

"My friends," he said, "I asked you here this evening not only for the great pleasure of your company, but to tell you something which I feel you should be the first to know. After all, you were all connected in one way or another with the late Lord Charlton, and you all know the circumstances of his most recent will, and the job with which I was entrusted. Well, I am delighted to tell you that my mission had been accomplished. I have found Simon Warwick."

The announcement was greeted in silence. Bertie Hamstone, who knew already and had told his wife, Elizabeth, merely settled back into his chair and fiddled with the band of his cigar. The other guests, however, sat up tensely, waiting for details.

Ambrose went on. "I say that I am delighted, and of course I am in the sense that it was Lord Charlton's dearest wish that his nephew should inherit. He wanted, I think, both to make up for his previous indifference to his brother's son, and also to make sure that control of the Warwick businesses remained in family hands."

At that, Sir Percy Crumble let out something very like a snort, and Lady Diana started to say something and then thought better of it.

"Now," said Ambrose, "as I said, we are all involved in some way. Bertie and I, of course, are the executors of the will. We have agreed to submit the evidence which we have collected to a court of law, and have it legally recognized that our candidate is, in fact, Simon Warwick. I may say that, in my view, the evidence is incontestable. You agree, Bertie?"

Bertram Hamstone, florid and fifty and a pillar of a small but exclusive London bank, grunted his assent.

Ambrose went on. "As for the rest of you, I am afraid this may not come as tidings of great joy. Cecily, as we all know, spent her life in Alexander Warwick's service, acting as his confidential secretary for more than thirty years."

He smiled warmly down the table at Cecily Smeed. She gave him an angry little nod, displaying the unbending lack of emotion that had intimidated not only her inferiors at Warwick Industries, but many of her nominal superiors as well. She was a tall, handsome woman in her fifties—gray haired, beautifully groomed, certainly not dowdy. Just formidable.

"Under Lord Charlton's previous will," Ambrose continued relentlessly, "Cecily Smeed stood to inherit . . . a sizable sum. Under the present will, she gets the silver inkwell which always stood on Lord Charlton's desk, and which he hopes she will keep as a memento of her work with him."

The look which Cecily Smeed directed at Ambrose would have reduced most men to quivering silence, but Ambrose did not appear to notice it. At least, it checked the irreverent giggle which Rosalie hastily suppressed. She had never liked Cecily Smeed, and had always been afraid of her.

"Sir Percy and Lady Diana," Ambrose went on, "are in a different position. As managing director of Warwick Industries, Sir Percy has virtually been running the whole concern for years. His chairman of the board, Lord Charlton, was elderly and in failing health, and was prepared to delegate his authority. It remains to be seen what Simon Warwick, as principal shareholder, will do. I realize that the coming months are bound to be an anxious time for all top executive management in the group."

Surprisingly, Sir Percy gave a booming laugh. "Noon o' your bizness, yoong Quince," he said, giving full rein to his thick North Country accent. Percy Crumble had risen through the ranks of Warwick Industries, and it took more than a milksop of a London lawyer to rattle him. For all his Savile Row suits and aristocratic wife, Percy Crumble was still essentially the lean, shrewd, quick-witted young man who had nipped up the career ladder by a combination of hard work, acumen, and complete ruthlessness.

Ambrose smiled and bowed briefly in his direction. "I realize that, Sir Percy," he said. "I just thought that everybody here should know all the facts." He paused, and changed gears. "As for my friend Denton Westbury, I am afraid the picture is not bright. As you may know, Lord Charlton agreed several years ago to the appointment of Denton as president of the Charlton Foundation, which was to administer the very considerable charitable funds resulting from Lord Charlton's bequests. He and I have been working together for quite some time, making all preparations so that the foundation could come into being as soon as possible after Lord Charlton's death. Denton, dear boy, I very much fear that you are out of a job."

Denton Westbury smiled—a smile that, like the rest of him, was short and thin. "That has always been a possibility, Ambrose," he said.

"A possibility, yes. Now it seems to be an inevitability."

Rosalie Quince frowned. It seemed to her that Ambrose was being unnecessarily spiteful. The party had been given simply to give these people advance news of the discovery of Simon Warwick. The fact that neither she nor Ambrose particularly liked any of them was neither here nor there.

"Well," said Ambrose, "there you have it. Forewarned is forearmed. All of us around this table are going to have to adjust . . . first, to the fact that Simon Warwick exists, and secondly, to the man himself. I think we should drink a toast. To Simon Warwick."

He raised his glass. There was dead silence. It was Percy Crumble who voiced the spirit of the meeting when, instead of drinking, he said bluntly, " 'Oo is the bastard?"

Ambrose grinned broadly, and at once the atmosphere relaxed and became almost conspiratorial.

"He's a man in his thirties," he said, "who currently goes by the name of Simon Finch. Through the good offices of an English solicitor called Alfred Humberton, he was privately adopted in 1944 after the death of his parents by a Captain and Mrs. Finch. Captain Finch was an American soldier married to an English girl, and Simon traveled to the United States with them, as their child, at the end of 1944. However, at the age of fifteen he ran away from home and returned to England. He is now completely Anglicized—you would never take him for an American. He is unmarried, and he strikes me as being shy and somewhat nervous, but not stupid. I can't see him planning any forceful takeover of the affairs of Warwick Industries. I think that you will be able to work harmoniously with him, Sir Percy."

Cecily Smeed said, "Are you absolutely convinced, Mr. Quince, that you have the right man?"

"The evidence is all there," said Ambrose. "That is—all except one small detail, which I intend to sort out in my office on Saturday morning."

"What's that? What detail?" Diana Crumble leaned forward across the table, her long, thin face thrust toward Ambrose.

Easily, Ambrose said, "This has all been completely confidential up to now, but in fact there have been two claimants whom I was forced to take seriously. One was Simon Finch. He is most certainly our man. He was able to produce not only the accurate story of his life, which has been corroborated by independent witnesses in the United States, but also all the relevant documents—except one—which he took with him when he ran away from home."

"What documents?" demanded Sir Percy.

"Letters from Humberton to the Finches arranging details of the adoption."

"Could they have been forged?"

"I'm afraid not, Sir Percy. They are written on Humberton's dye-stamped office stationery, and an expert has confirmed that the paper is at least thirty years old. Even more conclusive, among Lord Charlton's personal papers I chanced upon a letter from Humberton, written in 1943 on a different matter altogether. There is no doubt that it was typed on the same machine."

"Hm." Sir Percy grunted. "But you say one document is missing. What is it?"

"The passport which was issued to the infant Simon Warwick to enable him to leave England with the Finches in 1944."

"Well, it was probably—"

Ambrose held up his hand. "You misunderstand me, Sir Percy. I did not say that it was missing. It is, in fact, in the possession of the other claimant. That was why I had to investigate him seriously. However, once Rosalie and I got to America and started making inquiries, it was easy enough to blow his story to shreds. He is a brash, forceful, plausible young man named Harold Benson, Jr. And I may say," Ambrose added with a smile, "that if I were connected with Warwick Industries, I would be extremely glad that I was not going to have him as my chairman of the board. Happily, there is no fear of that."

"But how did he get hold of the passport?" asked Cecily.

"I don't know," said Ambrose, "but I intend to find out. The two families lived not too far from each other in Virginia, and the boys were the same age. Personally, I am convinced that they knew each other, and that Benson somehow acquired the passport from Finch. Until today, neither knew of the other's claim. Each thought that I had gone to America solely to investigate him. However, I have a little surprise lined up for ten o'clock on Saturday morning. I have invited both young men to come to my office in order to confront a rival candidate. I am quite sure that they will recognize each other, and in the shock of that moment I shall be able to find out exactly what happened to that passport. It is the final piece of the jigsaw."

Elizabeth and Bertram Hamstone were the last to leave the dinner party. At the front door, Hamstone took Ambrose by the arm, and said, "You certainly let them have it from the shoulder, Ambrose."

Ambrose shrugged. "No point in mincing words. They have to know, and make up their minds to accept the situation. I'm sorry for Cecily and Denton. Percy's as tough as old boots. He won't have any trouble disposing of poor Mr. Finch."

Susan Benedict, Ambrose Quince's secretary, arrived at the offices of Quince, Quince, Quince and Quince at nine o'clock on Saturday morning. She opened up the main door from the corridor, and then the door into Ambrose's own suite. She took off her coat and hung it up in the outermost office, which was her own domain. Then she walked through the waiting room and into Ambrose's office, where she satisfied herself that all was in order before unlocking the door that led directly onto the corridor, and that was marked PRIVATE on the outside.

Susan was a tall blonde with a round, babyish face, who traveled

49

up to town every morning from Wimbledon, where she shared a flat with two other girls. She had been romantically and hopelessly in love with Ambrose ever since she had come to work for Quince, Quince, Quince and Quince as a junior typist, five years ago. Her first promotion had been to the post of secretary to Mr. Silverstein, but by cautious maneuvering she had inveigled herself into the job of Ambrose's secretary when Miss Bunting—who had worked for forty years for Ambrose's father—finally doddered into reluctant retirement.

Ambrose knew perfectly well that Susan Benedict was in love with him, and used the fact to his advantage. After all, he had never encouraged the girl in any way—and she must know that she never had a chance against the dark, nubile, intelligent Rosalie. From a practical point of view, however, the situation had great benefits. Miss Benedict was never too busy to stay and work late at the office—by herself, naturally. Miss Benedict was only too ready to do a little shopping for Ambrose (it was really for Rosalie, but that fact was never mentioned) during her lunch hour. Above all, Miss Benedict was only too pleased to come in on Saturday mornings, when Ambrose frequently liked to talk with clients in the quiet atmosphere of an almost deserted office building. Ambrose always insisted that Miss Benedict should be compensated for Saturday work, either with extra money or time off; Susan ritually refused both, but occasionally indulged in the luxury of a protracted lunch hour when her mother came up from the country on a shopping trip. She persisted in regarding these few-and-far-between leaves of absence during office hours as a tremendous favor, whereas in fact they were considerably less than her due. As Rosalie often remarked to friends, Ambrose had an absolute treasure of a secretary.

Susan returned to her own office and sat down at the desk. She glanced at her watch. Only ten past nine. The two clients were not due until ten o'clock, and Ambrose would arrive even later. There was, as Susan knew, an element of one-upmanship in keeping people waiting. Pent in the small, gloomy waiting room—little more than a corridor linking Susan's office with Ambrose's—clients became nervous and irritated and therefore malleable. They would not realize that Ambrose was merely late, for he would go directly into his office through the door marked PRIVATE, and then buzz through to Susan that he was ready for his appointment.

Susan would then open the door to the waiting room and announce, "Mr. Quince will see you now." Whereupon, like a carefully rehearsed double act, Ambrose himself would open the door at the far end of the waiting room, which led to his office, and come forward, welcoming hand outstretched.

"How nice to see you, Mr. Blank. So sorry I had to keep you waiting. Do come in."

The client was left with the impression that vital work had prevented Ambrose from leaving his desk any sooner, and he also felt subtly flattered that such a busy and important man should come to the office door personally to welcome him. It was a good system, and Susan thoroughly approved of it.

Meanwhile, she decided to get on with some typing, which could easily have waited until Monday. She would, in fact, have been more usefully employed in going on with the knitting that she kept in her lower desk drawer, but she, too, believed in creating an impression. She intended to be busy with office work when the clients arrived. In that way, she could contrive to keep them waiting until she finished a line of typing. As far as possible, Susan modeled herself on Ambrose.

Actually, she had only been at work for about ten minutes when there was a tentative knock on the door that led from the main office of Quince, Quince, Quince and Quince. Susan stopped typing for long enough to call, "Come in!" and then resumed with intense concentration. The door opened, and a tall, gangling man with light brown hair and blue eyes came in, hesitantly. Susan recognized him from previous visits.

"Good morning," he said nervously.

Susan finished a line, whipped the paper crisply from the machine, glanced it over, and then looked up. "Good morning, Mr. Finch. You're very early."

"Yes, I am a little," Finch admitted guiltily.

"Your appointment isn't until ten o'clock, you know. Mr. Quince isn't in yet."

"Er . . . half-past nine, actually," murmured Simon Finch.

Susan flipped open her engagement book. "Ten o'clock," she said.

"I . . . em . . . I had a message, you know. Nine-thirty . . ."

Susan had lost interest. "Please take a seat in the waiting room. I'll let you know when Mr. Quince can see you."

"Thank you very much," said Simon Finch, humbly. He went into the waiting room and closed the door behind him. Susan attacked the typewriter with renewed vigor. It gave her a certain amount of satisfaction to think of Mr. Finch sitting for over half an hour with nothing to divert him but a year-old *National Geographic* magazine.

She was almost running out of material to type when, at ten o'clock on the dot, her office door opened and Harold Benson walked in. Susan looked up and smiled. She had taken to Mr. Benson the very first time he came to the office. So beautifully dressed, and such an assured, well-bred manner, even if he was an American.

"Good morning, Miss Benedict," he said.

Typical of him, Susan thought, to have taken the trouble to find out her name. She said, "Good morning, Mr. Benson. Do take a seat in the waiting room. Mr. Finch is there already."

Harold Benson stood quite still for a moment. Then he said, "Did you say Mr. Finch?"

"That's right. He got here ever so early. I'll let you know as soon as Mr. Quince can see you."

Without a word, Benson went into the waiting room to join Simon Finch. Susan waited until the door was closed, and then pressed the buzzer that rang in Ambrose's office. He had not buzzed her, so she was virtually certain that he had not yet arrived—but just in case, she tried. As she had expected, there was no reply.

It was perhaps a minute later that the door of the waiting room burst open, and Harold Benson came stumbling out, white faced. He gasped, "Miss Benedict . . . police . . . call the police . . ."

"Why, Mr. Benson, whatever's the matter?"

Benson gesticulated toward the waiting room. "Dead . . . there's a dead man in there . . ."

Susan did not lose her aplomb. "I'm sure you must be mistaken, Mr. Benson. That's Mr. Finch."

"I don't care who he is, he's dead!" shouted Benson, who seemed to be recovering from his shock. "Go and look for yourself!"

Susan Benedict was not squeamish. With no hesitation, she went into the waiting room, with Benson hovering at her back. Sure enough, Simon Finch was slumped in one of the two armchairs, his head lolling unnaturally and his face horribly contorted. It was perfectly obvious that he had been strangled, and that he was extremely dead. The morning edition of the *Times* was scattered on the floor around him.

"Oh, my goodness," said Susan, who was not a great phrasemaker. "We must tell Mr. Quince!" She ran to the door to

Ambrose's office, and opened it, just as Ambrose came in from the corridor.

"Good morning, Susan," he said. Then, "Whatever's the matter?"

"Oh, Mr. Quince, I don't know what to do! It's Mr. Finch. Somebody's killed him!"

Ambrose was always at his best in an emergency. Having inspected what remained of Simon Finch, and having satisfied himself that the poor fellow was really dead, he very competently set about telephoning Scotland Yard and his own doctor. He admonished Susan Benedict and Harold Benson not to touch anything, and when they both attempted to pour out their accounts of what had happened, he told them sternly that they must not discuss the matter with anybody except the police. Then he firmly closed both doors to the waiting room, and took Susan and Benson into his own office to await the arrival of the law.

Susan, full of adoring admiration for Mr. Quince's handling of the situation, began to feel very much better and volunteered to go down to the café on the corner and get them all a nice cup of coffee. Ambrose, however, vetoed the idea.

"I don't think *any* of us should leave the office," he said, with a meaning look at Harold Benson. However, he did telephone to the coffee shop and ask them to send three cups up—a service that they were glad to perform if they were not too busy. The boy, Ambrose was careful to say, should come straight into his office through the door marked PRIVATE.

So it was that Ambrose Quince, Susan Benedict, and Harold Benson, Jr., were sipping hot black coffee in silence when a police siren in the street below announced the arrival of Chief Superintendent Henry Tibbett of the CID, together with Detective Inspector Derek Reynolds, a police doctor and an ambulance crew, a photographer and a fingerprint expert, and all the panoply of a murder-investigation team. The thought uppermost in Ambrose's mind at that moment was not pity for Simon Finch or distress that a murder should have taken place in his office; it was the realization that Simon Warwick would never come into his inheritance. He remembered the remarks he had made at his dinner party. All the people around that table might be said to have had a motive for murder. Most of all, over the rim of his coffee cup, he studied Harold Benson, Jr. If that man imagined, thought Ambrose, that Simon Finch's death would somehow assist his own claim to be Simon Warwick, then he had another swift think coming.

6

Ambrose greeted Henry with a mixture of relief and enthusiasm.

"Chief Superintendent Tibbett! What a very fortunate chance. I am afraid this is a very distressing business."

"Sudden death always is," said Henry. "Especially if it appears to be murder, as I gather it does."

"Well, you can see for yourself," Ambrose said. "It's pretty obvious the poor fellow was strangled, and it's hard to see how that could have been accidental or self-inflicted. Your medical experts will be able to determine exactly what happened, of course, but my guess is that he was knocked unconscious and then throttled. Probably a karate chop to the back of the ear. Oh, please don't think I've touched anything. I'm giving you my opinion just on what I saw."

"Well . . ." said Henry, with deliberate vagueness. "Well, I'll go and take a look at the body, and then come back here and you can introduce me to your friends."

"I'm terribly sorry, old man. This is Miss Susan Benedict, my secretary. And this is Mr. Harold Benson, who"—Ambrose paused significantly—"who found the body. Chief Superintendent Henry Tibbett of the CID."

Henry said, "I'm delighted to meet you both. I'll be back in a minute." He went quickly through the door that separated Ambrose's office from the waiting room.

The small, passagelike room was full of people. Photographers were taking pictures and fingerprint experts were busy with powder and brushes. Simon Finch's body lay in exactly the same position as when Ambrose had seen it. A photographer's arc lamp now bathed it in a pool of white light, but pending Henry's arrival nothing had been touched.

Henry studied the late Simon Finch, aware of the mixture of compassion and respect that he always felt in the presence of a creature dead by violence—whether it be a murdered human being or a cat hit by a car and thrown into a ditch. In the final, complete, and utter vulnerability of death, there was always the silent dignity, the paradoxical invulnerability of a being beyond pain or inquisition or any human power. For a moment, Henry was swept by a sense of the futility of his job, of all these busy people swarming like ants over the corpse. The man was dead. What did it matter who had killed him? Beside the simple fact of death, nothing seemed important. Then he pulled himself together. Of course it was important to find out who had killed this young man. Apart from any question of abstract justice, a person who has killed once may kill again.

Henry looked carefully at the body, and at the scattered pages of newspaper around it. He said to the photographer, "You've got all this?"

"Yes, sir."

"Okay. Inspector Reynolds, let's have everything out of his pockets—protected for fingerprinting. Then you can take a look at him, Doctor, and take him away for an autopsy."

The police doctor smiled wryly. "I should have thought even you could see that the man had been strangled, Tibbett."

Henry said, "Expertly?"

"Depends what you mean by that. I should say he was knocked unconscious first. After that, it's just a matter of applying pressure. We'll let you know for certain soon. Finished, Reynolds? Good. We'll keep the clothes for analysis, of course. Okay, chaps. Get him on the stretcher."

On the table, beside the pile of *National Geographic* magazines, Inspector Reynolds laid out the contents of the dead man's pockets—each item encased in transparent plastic. It was not a large collection. There was a key ring with a couple of latchkeys on it; a clean white handkerchief; the return half of a railway ticket from Westbourne to London, cheap day-return fare; and a letter from Ambrose Quince addressed to Simon Finch, Esq., 4 Seaview Gardens, Westbourne, Sussex. The letter was in crisp legalese, and requested Mr. Finch to be at Mr. Quince's office at 10 A.M. on Saturday, January 14, in order to confront a rival claimant to the estate due to Simon Warwick. There was also an imitation-leather wallet containing eight pounds in notes and a few postage stamps. Apart from 35p. in small change and a checkbook from the Sussex National Bank, Westbourne branch, there was nothing else.

Henry said, "Secretive sort of chap."

Reynolds grinned. "Fishy, if you ask me, sir. No driver's license, no visiting cards, no nothing. Like as if his pockets had been spring-cleaned."

"Maybe they were," said Henry. "At any rate we have a name and an address, and Mr. Quince obviously knew him. You take over in here, Reynolds. I'll have a word with the people next door."

Ambrose Quince was slightly taken aback when he realized that he was not going to be the first to be interviewed. Henry's quick and smooth explanation that he wanted to talk first to Miss Benedict, as she must have been the first to arrive at the office that morning, seemed a little thin to Ambrose. He felt that priority should go to seniority rather than to punctuality. However, he put a gracious face on things and allowed Henry to lead Susan off to the outer office, which had been set aside for interviewing.

Susan, pleased at being picked first and very much at ease, explained smilingly to Henry that she was Mr. Quince's private secretary, and that there was nothing at all unusual about Mr. Quince receiving clients on Saturday morning.

"It's always nice and quiet," she explained, "and Mr. Quince isn't being bothered with phone calls and so on. I'm always glad to come in on a Saturday if Mr. Quince wants me. It's no trouble. Besides, he's ever so generous about giving me time off to compensate."

She described accurately and concisely the arrival of Mr. Finch. "Ever so early. Twenty past nine for a ten o'clock appointment. I told him he'd have to wait."

Henry said, "He had to come up to London from Westbourne. I suppose there wasn't a later train that he could conveniently catch."

"I don't know about that," said Susan. "I think he was just muddleheaded. Said something about a nine-thirty appointment. Well, that's nonsense. It's down here in my book for ten."

"Can you remember exactly what he said?"

Susan frowned. "Not really. I didn't pay much attention—I wanted to get on with my typing. Oh, I think he mumbled something about a message, now I come to think of it."

Henry was interested. "You mean, he said he had received a message changing the time of his appointment?"

"I don't know what he said. I wasn't really listening."

"Please try to remember, Miss Benedict. It could be important."

There was a pause, and then Susan said, "Well, all I can say is that I've a vague sort of recollection of him using the word 'message.' And I do know that he seemed to imagine he was expected at nine-thirty."

"That's very helpful, Miss Benedict. So you showed him into the waiting room and went on with your work."

"I didn't exactly show him in. He knew where to go."

"You had met Mr. Finch before, had you, Miss Benedict?"

"Oh, yes."

"Here in the office, or socially?"

"Oh, only in the office, of course." Susan sounded disdainful.

"Can you tell me what his business was with Mr. Quince?"

Susan's eyebrows went up. "You mean you don't know?"

"I know nothing except that I've been sent to investigate a murder in Mr. Quince's waiting room," said Henry.

With a good story to tell, Susan became voluble. "Why, Mr. Finch and Mr. Benson are the two claimants to Lord Charlton's will. They both say they're Simon Warwick. Mr. Quince went off to America to make inquiries about them, and when he came back he wrote to both of them arranging this meeting. You see, up till then each one of them thought he was the only claimant."

"There aren't any others?" Henry asked.

"Not serious. Just a few crackpot letters—you know."

Henry said, "When Mr. Quince came back from America, did he tell you which claimant he fancied to be genuine?"

Susan hesitated for a moment, then shook her head. "No, he didn't tell me anything. Just dictated a letter to each of them—exactly the same letter—telling them to be here this morning to confront a rival claimant." She gave a little laugh. "Actually, Chief Superintendent, I don't think there's any doubt about it, myself."

"You don't?"

"Well, I mean, just ask yourself. First of all, little Simon Warwick was adopted by an American couple, but Mr. Finch was English as English. And then—well, Simon Warwick was the nephew of a lord, after all. You can see—I mean, you could see that Mr. Finch wasn't out of the top drawer, if you know what I mean. But Mr. Benson, now—well, he's different altogether. He's American all right, and yet with it he's a really superior sort of person. He's Simon Warwick all right."

"And yet," Henry said, "it was Simon Finch who was murdered. I wonder why."

"Don't ask *me*," said Susan, with distaste. "I suppose somebody didn't like him."

"That seems obvious," said Henry.

His light irony was lost on Miss Benedict. She sniffed and said, "He's the sort of person who would get murdered. I just wish he hadn't done it in Mr. Quince's waiting room."

Henry let this pass. He said, "Right. Where were we?" He glanced at his notebook. "Mr. Finch arrived at twenty past nine, and went into the waiting room. What happened next?"

"Nothing happened. I went on with my typing."

"You didn't hear any sound from the waiting room?"

"Of course not. If I had, I'd have gone in to see what was happening. But I was typing fast, you see, and that makes enough noise so that I wouldn't have heard anything through the door unless it had been really loud."

Henry nodded. "I see. So what was the next thing that did happen?"

"Mr. Benson. He came just at ten, on the dot. He didn't make any silly mistakes about his appointment. We exchanged a few words, and then he went into the waiting room."

"Can you remember what was said?"

"Oh, nothing special, Just 'good morning.' And I told him that Mr. Finch was here already, and asked him to wait. That's all."

Henry said, "So Mr. Benson went to join Mr. Finch in the waiting room. And then?"

"Well, I was pretty sure that Mr. Quince hadn't arrived, because he hadn't buzzed through to me, but I buzzed his office just in case he was there."

"What's all this buzzing?" Henry asked, and Susan explained the office communications system.

"And then," she went on, "poor Mr. Benson came running out of the waiting room, terribly upset, and told me Mr. Finch was dead. I went in with him to have a look, and there he was—Mr. Finch, I mean. Luckily just then Mr. Quince arrived, and of course he took over and then everything was all right."

Henry said, "You buzzed Mr. Quince's office after Mr. Benson had gone into the waiting room?"

"Yes. I told you."

"So some time elapsed before Mr. Benson came running out to tell you he had found the body?"

Susan was instantly on the defensive. "It doesn't take much time to buzz."

"And to get no reply?"

"Mr. Benson came out of there just as quick as he could."

"Miss Benedict," said Henry, "that waiting room is fairly small, and nobody could miss the sight of a dead body in the middle of it. Doesn't it strike you as strange that Mr. Benson even went in at all? Wouldn't he have seen Finch's body from the doorway?"

Definitely upset, Susan said, "It wasn't more than a moment. I expect he just looked to see . . . maybe he thought Mr. Finch was just ill . . ."

"Maybe he did. Now, please Miss Benedict—tell me exactly how long Mr. Benson was in that room, in your estimation."

"I . . . I don't know. Perhaps a minute."

"With the door shut behind him?"

"Well . . . yes. But it swings shut."

"Only a minute?"

"Well . . . it could have been a little longer. I don't know. I was doing my typing . . ." Susan was badly rattled. "There'll be an explanation. Just ask Mr. Benson."

"I propose," said Henry, "to do just that. Please wait in Mr. Quince's office for a little longer, will you, Miss Benedict?"

Harold Benson, Jr., was still in a state of tightly controlled shock when he arrived in the outer office to be interviewed. He confirmed in a quiet voice the simple facts about his letter from Ambrose Quince and his arrival at the office.

Henry interrupted to say, "I understand this meeting was to bring you face to face with a rival claimant to Lord Charlton's estate?"

Benson flushed. "That's what Quince said in his letter. I knew, of course, that the other man must be a fraud."

"Because you are Simon Warwick?"

"Because I am Simon Warwick."

"So you had nothing to fear from this obvious impostor?"

Benson shifted uncomfortably in his chair. He said, "I knew that he couldn't be Simon Warwick, but I didn't know what sort of claim he could possibly have made that would make Quince take him seriously. So of course I was a little worried. I was also very curious."

Henry said, "All right. Let's get on. You went into the waiting room, closing the door behind you. Didn't you see the body at once?"

"Of course I did."

"Then—"

"That's to say, I saw this character sitting in the corner. Miss Benedict had told me that Mr. Finch had already arrived. I thought it was odd, because he appeared to be asleep."

"Asleep?"

"Yeah. He was lying back in the armchair, with his newspaper over his face. I said, 'Good morning,' and he didn't say anything. So I sat down, and looked at him again, and I thought, 'There's something mightly peculiar about that guy. Could be he's ill or passed out or something.' So I went over and shook him by the shoulder and said, 'Hey, Mr. Finch'—and he just fell forward onto the floor, and the newspaper flew all around everywhere, and of course I could see then that he was dead. I was—well, I was appalled. I just rushed out and called Miss Benedict, and—well, I guess you know the rest."

"Mr. Benson," Henry said, "had you ever met Mr. Finch before this morning?"

"Of course not."

"You didn't know him, even by sight?"

"Certainly not. I tell you, I didn't even know of his existence until I got Quince's letter."

"Very well, Mr. Benson. Please leave your address with Inspector Reynolds. You'll be staying in England for some time, I hope?"

"You're darned right I will. I'm staying until this business gets good and sorted out."

"The murder, you mean?"

Benson looked surprised. "The murder? Hell, no. The will."

"You don't think that what happened this morning—?"

"What happened this morning," said Benson angrily, "was a damn nuisance, but it was nothing to do with me. This guy who called himself Simon Finch—somebody obviously didn't like him, and I'm not surprised, if he went around pressing fraudulent claims. So somebody killed him. That makes no difference to the fact that I am Simon Warwick, and I came over here to claim my inheritance, and by God I'm going to do it."

Henry said, "You must surely realize that you are in an awkward position, Mr. Benson. According to Miss Benedict, Mr. Finch went into the waiting room shortly before half-past nine. She was in the outer office all the time, and nobody else went in there until you did. And you were in there an appreciable time before—"

"I've already explained that," said Benson. "And I'd like to point out that this isn't a locked-room mystery, Chief Superintendent. You must have noticed that there's a door from Quince's office into the waiting room and another out into the corridor—and they were both unlocked. Anybody could have walked in anytime between nine-thirty and ten and killed that guy and walked out again. I just had the bad luck to find him."

Henry said, "You know a lot about the office layout, Mr. Benson."

"So does anybody who's ever visited Quince. You're ushered in via Miss Benedict and the waiting room, and when you leave, Quince shoots you straight out into the corridor from his office."

There was a little pause. Then Henry said, "By the way, did you have a newspaper with you when you arrived here this morning?"

"No, I didn't. I glanced at one over breakfast at the hotel, but I didn't bring it with me."

When Harold Benson had gone, Henry—to Ambrose Quince's mounting annoyance—asked Susan to come back into the office. She was most emphatic that Mr. Benson had not been carrying a newspaper. When it came to Mr. Finch, however, she hesitated.

"Well, he must have had one, mustn't he, because it was all over the place. This morning's *Times*. And since Mr. Benson didn't have one—"

"There wouldn't have been a copy in the waiting room for clients to read?"

"Oh, no. Definitely not. So it must have been Mr. Finch's."

Henry said, "You don't sound absolutely sure, Miss Benedict."

"Well, I am." Susan moved to the offensive. "Now I come to think of it, I remember distinctly. He had a newspaper under his arm."

Henry sighed. "Very well."

"Can I go now?"

"You can go back to the other office. Don't leave the building."

Ambrose Quince was brisk, businesslike, and in a curious way seemed to Henry to be almost pleased by the turn of events. He described his arrival at the office at five past ten—"Does them no harm to let them cool their heels for a few minutes"—his encounter with Susan and Benson, and the subsequent steps he had taken. Then he said, "Well, it all seems quite straightforward, doesn't it, Tibbett?"

"How do you mean?"

Ambrose gave a little laugh. "I'm sorry. I should have put you in the picture sooner. The fact is that Simon Finch was the real Simon Warwick, beyond any shadow of doubt. I have a file in my office—naturally you'll want to inspect it—which proves conclusively that we had found our missing heir. As a matter of fact, I gave a little dinner party at my house last week for the various people most closely concerned with Lord Charlton's will, and told them that I was convinced that we had the right man, and that I intended to submit proof of his identity to a court of law."

Henry said, "Did you also tell them that your claimant was coming here this morning?"

"Yes, I did. I told them that I intended to dispose of Mr. Harold Benson once and for all by confronting him with Simon Finch. For reasons which you will see when you study the file, I am convinced that Benson knew Finch as a boy and somehow got the passport from him."

"The passport?"

"It's all there in the file, Tibbett. Just take it from me that Finch was Simon Warwick and that Harold Benson is a very inefficient impostor. He possessed just one piece of purely circumstantial evidence to support his claim, and I suppose he hoped that Finch wouldn't come forward with counter-evidence. When he got my letter and realized that we had rumbled him, he decided to take drastic action."

"Really?" said Henry.

Quince appeared not to notice the interruption. He said, "Susan must have told you that Finch was under the impression that his appointment with me had been changed to half-past nine. Somebody must have got that message to him, and it's obvious that the somebody was Benson. He made sure that Finch would get here well ahead of him, thus leaving a decent time interval in which somebody else *might* have done the killing. Then he arrived himself and did the job. Wouldn't take any time for a man who knew what he was doing. Bertie Hamstone was a Commando during the war, and he's often told me how quickly and quietly you could dispose of a man. Chop and choke, he calls it. As soon as I saw

Finch, I remembered what he'd said."

"Bertie Hamstone?"

"My fellow executor on Charlton's will. Banker at Sprott's. Anyhow, Tibbett, if Benson believes that the field is clear now that his rival is out of the way, he is wrong. I have the proof that the late Simon Finch was in fact the late Simon Warwick, and I shall get that fact duly attested."

Henry said, "And what will happen to the money?"

"Lord Charlton was quite definite on that point," said Ambrose. "If Simon Warwick should be found to have died, the money would go to his eldest legitimate child. If he had no child, then we revert to the previous will. The money goes to charity. According to what he told me—and of course you'll have to check this out—Simon Finch was unmarried. Therefore, the original will comes back into force, and many worthy causes will be the gainers."

"All the money goes to charity, does it, Mr. Quince?"

"Oh, there are a few personal bequests . . . the largest is to Charlton's personal secretary . . . his butler and chauffeur get a few thousand . . ."

"And even those bequests are canceled under the new will?"

"I'm afraid so," said Ambrose. "I tried to persuade him to let them stand, but he was adamant."

"Just for the record," Henry said, "what about you, Mr. Quince? Was there a bequest to you under the old will?"

Ambrose grinned. "Certainly not, worse luck. No, I get my fee as executor and that's that. Whoever the beneficiaries may be."

"Well," Henry said, "I'd be grateful if you'd let me take away your file on Simon Warwick—that is, all the information you have on Simon Finch and Harold Benson. I'd also like a copy of the original will and a guest list of your dinner party."

Ambrose looked taken aback. "Surely you're not suggesting—?" The same thought had occurred to him, but he had not expected Henry to latch on to it quite so fast.

"I'm not suggesting anything," said Henry. "Just trying to get a complete picture. By the way, Mr. Quince, did you bring a copy of the *Times* to the office with you this morning?"

"Yes." Ambrose was surprised. "I always do. I buy one every morning off the old newsvendor on the corner."

"Do you still have it?"

"It must be in my office. If you'd care to look—"

"Yes, if you don't mind, Mr. Quince. I'd like to."

Ambrose gave Henry a quizzical look, but all he said was, "Better go via the corridor. I think your chaps are still busy in the waiting room."

Susan Benedict and Harold Benson were sitting in Ambrose's office, chatting and looking considerably more relaxed now that their interviews with the police were over, at least for the time being. However, they stopped talking abruptly as Ambrose and Henry came into the room. On the desk between them lay an unopened copy of the *Times*.

"There it is," said Ambrose. "Just where I left it. I remember now putting it down on the desk before I went into the waiting room."

Instinctively, all eyes went to the newspaper. Then Henry said, "So the paper which was all over the waiting room must have been Mr. Finch's."

"Or Mr. Benson's," said Ambrose, without looking at Harold.

Easily, Henry said, "Miss Benedict seems to recall that you weren't carrying a newspaper when you arrived this morning, Mr. Benson. Is that correct?"

Susan nodded vigorously, and Benson said, "Quite correct. I told you already."

"Then it must have been Finch's," Ambrose said.

"Or somebody's," said Henry. "Well, I don't think I need detain you gentlemen any longer. We have your addresses, and I'm afraid we shall have to bother you again, so don't leave town without letting us know. And now I'd like a final word with Miss Benedict."

"Again?" Ambrose did not sound pleased.

"Just to cross-check a couple of points," said Henry, with an amiable vagueness that deceived nobody.

Quince and Benson glared at each other and took their leave, Ambrose standing back with exaggerated politeness to let the American go through the door first. Then he paused and said, "You'll lock up as usual, will you, Susan?"

Henry said, "I'm afraid my people will be here for some time more, Mr. Quince. Fortunately tomorrow is Sunday. I hope that by Monday we can restore your office to you for normal working. Meanwhile, I'm afraid we must keep the keys."

"Oh, very well," said Ambrose. "The Chief Superintendent would like to take all the Simon Warwick files and a copy of Lord Charlton's original will, Susan. Please let him have them."

"Yes, Mr. Quince."

"As for the guest list," Ambrose added, "my wife will have all the details. Where should she send them?"

"If it's convenient," Henry said, "I could call this afternoon and pick them up. I have the address—in Ealing, isn't it?"

"Certainly, my dear fellow. It'll be a pleasure."

As soon as the door had closed behind Ambrose, Susan jumped up and said, "I'll get those files for you now, Chief Superintendent."

"In a moment, Miss Benedict. There's something I want to ask you first. Mr. Finch lived in Westbourne, didn't he?"

"That's right."

"You had his address and telephone number?"

"Yes, of course. It's all on the file. Well, it wasn't exactly a telephone number."

"Not a telephone number?"

"What I mean is, it wasn't his own telephone. He lived in a sort of boardinghouse, you see, and the landlady took messages if he wasn't in."

"I see. Now, I want you to think hard. Who knew Mr. Finch's telephone number?"

Susan frowned. "Well, I did, of course, and Mr. Quince could have got it from my book. And I suppose all Mr. Finch's friends in Westbourne and his family and—"

Henry held up his hand. "No, no," he said. "What I'm getting at is this. Did anybody outside this office ask you for Mr. Finch's number?"

"Oh, no. Well, that is, not really."

"What does that mean?"

"Well, you said 'outside this office,' and after all Mr. Hamstone's the other executor of Lord Charlton's will, which makes him—"

Henry said, "Mr. Hamstone of Sprott's Bank?"

"That's right. Mr. Bertram Hamstone. Such a nice gentleman. Well, him being the other executor, like I said, we're in touch with him a great deal. It must have been the day before yesterday, Mr. Hamstone's office called and asked for Mr. Finch's telephone number. They had his address, you see, but no phone number, and of course it wouldn't be in the book under Finch, not being his own telephone."

Henry said, "You say that Mr. Hamstone's office called. What does that mean? Whom did you actually speak to?"

"Oh, I don't know his name. A man. Sounded a bit like an

American—there's a lot of them work at Sprott's. He just said he was Mr. Hamstone's office and could I give him Mr. Finch's number."

"And you did."

"Well, of course. It wasn't a secret, was it?"

"No," said Henry. "No, of course it wasn't. Well, if you can find me those files, you can get along home. I'm afraid this has been a distressing experience for you, Miss Benedict."

"Oh, not really." Susan was being brisk and efficient, as Mr. Quince would have wanted her to be. "After all, I didn't really know Mr. Finch. It wasn't as if it was a friend."

"That's the sensible way to look at it," said Henry, with a smile.

7

That afternoon, while Henry sat in his office studying the file on the Simon Warwick affair, Detective Inspector Derek Reynolds set off to drive down to Westbourne, while Detective Sergeant Hawthorn—the third member of Henry's personal team—set about trying to check who might have been seen going into the office building on Theobald's Road between nine and ten that morning.

Hawthorn had little success. It seemed that, since it was Saturday, neither the doorman nor the elevator attendant had been on duty. The front door was left open from 9 A.M. to 6 P.M. for the convenience of eccentrics like Ambrose Quince who chose to work on Saturdays. At six o'clock, the burglar alarms were set and the building locked until Monday morning.

The only crumb of evidence that Hawthorn could unearth came from the newspaper seller on the corner—a small, cheerful Cockney. He knew Mr. Quince well, and he'd sold him a paper that morning at the usual time, ten o'clock sharp. Regular as clockwork was Mr. Quince. Well, no, not *every* Saturday, but every weekday and quite often Saturdays as well, like this morning. Other than this small corroborative detail, Hawthorn drew a blank. Saturday morning was different. The weekday behavior patterns were broken. People were not in their accustomed places, and the street was full of strangers.

Inspector Reynolds had better luck. Even though the helpful sergeant at the Westbourne police station could tell him nothing about Simon Finch, he did recognize the address of Finch's lodgings. Yes, that was Mrs. Busby and he knew her quite well. Not that she'd ever been in trouble with the police—goodness me, no. A widow—a nice, motherly sort of woman. She let out rooms, mostly to single gentlemen. The sergeant knew her because she'd been into the station a couple of times—once when she was worried about one of her lodgers, a young boy who didn't show up for a couple of days, and another time to report her dog lost. Cocker spaniel, it was. Turned up on the beach the next day. The young man had turned up, too—he'd been in London on a spree. Well, Inspector Reynolds could see the sort of person she was—a kindly soul. She was certainly going to be upset when she heard about Mr. Finch.

The officer was right. Mrs. Busby sat in her neat front room, dabbing ineffectively at her eyes with a damp handkerchief, and repeating over and over again, "I can't believe it. Mr. Finch—dead and murdered! I just can't believe it."

"I'm afraid it's true, madam," said Reynolds. "That's why we're trying to find out all we can about him. I hope you can help us."

"Help you?" Mrs. Busby blew her nose—a small, pudgy nose now reddened with weeping, which sat like a cherry in the center of her pale, plump face. "I don't see how I can help you. I don't know anything about Mr. Finch."

"Well, for a start, how long had he been rooming with you?"

"Oh, not long. Not long at all. A matter of a few weeks. Just before Christmas it was, he came. Well, the beginning of December, like."

"Do you know what he did for a living?"

"I really couldn't tell you, Inspector. I did wonder at first if he might be a writer."

"What made you think that?" Reynolds asked.

"Well, for one thing he never seemed to have a regular job to go to—not an office, or anything like that. And then he'd be up in his room most of the day, hitting away at that great big typewriter."

"He's got a big typewriter in his room, has he?"

"Oh, not anymore. It was just before Christmas, I came downstairs one morning and found him in the hall, trying to open the front door with this great big machine in his arms. "Here, let me help you, Mr. Finch,' I said. 'Where are you going with that typewriter? Has it gone wrong?' 'No, Mrs. Busby,' he said. 'It's too big. I'm trading it for a smaller one.' Well, that seemed sensible to me. And sure enough he came back later in the day with a nice little portable. But after that he didn't seem to do so much writing. Well, it was Christmas, of course.''

Reynolds said, "Yes, tell me about Christmas. Did he go off and spend it with his family?"

Mrs. Busby shook her gray head sadly. "He didn't seem to have anybody in the world," she said. "Of course, I didn't like to pry. I just asked him if he'd be going home for Christmas, and he said no, he'd stay here. Well, it's a shame, isn't it? All my other young men went home—he was the only one left. I had him down here for Christmas dinner with my sister and her husband—but he only pecked at his food and hardly said a word."

Without much hope, Reynolds asked if Finch had had many friends to visit him. No, not one that Mrs. Busby could remember. Did he get much mail? Very little. Just a few typewritten letters that looked like they came from a lawyer's office. The same name over and over, if the inspector knew what she meant.

"Quince?" Reynolds asked.

"That's it. Quince and Quince and Quince and—I don't know how many, I'm sure. There were one or two catalogs and advertisements and that sort of thing. I don't remember any letters what you'd call personal."

"Telephone calls?"

"Just the one."

"When was that?"

"Let's see—where are we? Saturday today, isn't it? Yes, well then it must have been Thursday, round about lunchtime. Mr. Finch wasn't in. He'd go out every day around one o'clock to get something to eat. So I took the call."

"Please tell me about it as exactly as you can, Mrs. Busby."

"There's not much to tell. I picked up the telephone and said 'Hello,' and this voice asked to speak to Mr. Finch."

"Male or female voice?"

"Oh, it was a man all right. American, I'd say, although I can't be sure."

"So what did you say?"

"I said, 'I'm sorry, Mr. Finch is out having his lunch. I daresay he'll be in later if you want to call back.' But he said, 'No, no, that's not necessary. Can you take a message?' I said I could, and he said, 'I'm speaking for Mr. . . .' What was that name again?"

"Quince."

"That's right. Wait a minute—I wrote it down. Let's see if I can find it."

Mrs. Busby bustled out into the narrow hallway—Derek Reynolds reflected that she always seemed to move at a half run, as though late for an appointment. A minute later she was back, triumphantly waving a scrap of paper.

"Here it is. I daresay you'll want to keep it."

Reynolds read, penciled in neat script, the message: "Mr. Finch. Mr. Ambrose Quince's office rang. Please be there for your appointment on Saturday at 9:30, not 10. M. Busby."

"I take messages for my lodgers, you see," Mrs. Busby explained, "and I leave them in a little box by the telephone. They look in there as they come in, and if there's a message they generally take it away with them. But I happened to notice that Mr. Finch left his in the box. He must have read it, though, because I heard him leave the house really early this morning. I was just getting a cup of tea in the kitchen when I heard the front door bang, and saw him going past outside. 'Well,' I said to myself, 'he'll be catching the six o'clock up to London. Very wise. The six-thirty wouldn't really give him enough time to get to a nine-thirty appointment.' And now you come and tell me he's dead and gone . . . I can't believe it. I really can't."

Inspector Reynolds averted a new outburst of tears by requesting to see Mr. Finch's room. It was small, clean, and quite devoid of any personality. The new portable typewriter was there, and some typing paper and carbons, but no papers or correspondence except for Ambrose's letters, which were in a cardboard folder with QUINCE written on the outside. The wardrobe and chest of drawers contained a minimum of clean shirts, socks, and underwear, one pair of gray flannel trousers and a blazer, and a couple of inexpensive ties. The only books were a paperback of collected crossword puzzles and a heavy legal tome.

As Reynolds examined the latter, which appeared to concern itself with the laws of inheritance in the United Kingdom, Mrs. Busby, hovering at his shoulder, said, "He was a serious young man. Almost too serious, I'd say. But he paid regular."

"By cash or check?"

"Oh, always by check. He had an account at the Sussex National."

70

Reynolds put down the book, took another look at the portable typewriter, and then broke the bad news to Mrs. Busby that, in the absence of any traceable relatives, he would have to ask her to accompany him to London to identify the body. After an initial reaction of dismay, the prospect of a drive in a police car—"And we'll pay your fare back, of course"—seemed to cheer Mrs. Busby, and she promised to be ready when the inspector returned an hour later.

The inspector's next port of call, the bank, was predictably unfruitful. The establishment was closed, of course, it being a Saturday, but the local police had arranged for Inspector Reynolds to meet with the manager in his office. Simon Finch, it seemed, had opened his account on December 12 with a deposit of five hundred pounds in cash. No proof of his identity had been asked of him—it never was. Anybody might open an account in any name, and so long as it was in credit . . . No, there had been no further deposits. Withdrawals had consisted of a ten-pound weekly check to Mrs. Mary Busby, cash to the amount of fifty pounds, and twenty-five pounds fifty to Southern Typewriters, Ltd. The credit balance stood at three hundred and seventy-four pounds and fifty pence.

Southern Typewriters was a small shop on a side street, selling both new and used typewriters. The young man behind the counter remembered the transaction. Mr. Finch had bought a secondhand Remington portable in excellent condition—a great bargain at twenty-five fifty. Here was the sales slip. Paid by check. An old one in part exchange? No, nothing like that. Just a straightforward sale.

Derek Reynolds looked in again at the police station before he left Westbourne, and asked the local force to cooperate in trying to locate a large, elderly typewriter, probably an office model, which might have been pawned or traded recently. He had no real hope that anything would come of it. Then he went back to Seaview Gardens and picked up Mrs. Busby.

As he drove back to London, Reynolds diverted his mind from his passenger's chatter by rehearsing mentally the report that he would give to Chief Superintendent Tibbett.

The man's a phony. You take my word for it, sir, his name wasn't Simon Finch and he was almost certainly a petty villain. All the hallmarks are there—no papers, no friends, no family. This Finch thing is a new and temporary identity. Bank account and mail order catalogs to build it up, but nothing else. You run his mug through CRO, sir, and you'll find who he really was, or I'm a

Dutchman. As for the Simon Warwick thing—forget it. Funny, wasn't it, that the only book in his room was a legal work on the laws of inheritance. He's a phony, sir. Take it from me.

While Derek Reynolds and Mrs. Busby were still driving up the wet January roads from Westbourne to London, Henry Tibbett was sitting beside a comforting log fire in Ealing, sipping sherry and talking to Rosalie Quince. She was so sorry, she explained, but Ambrose had had to go out.

Rosalie frowned and smiled simultaneously—an attractive combination—and said, "A dull but important client is giving a cocktail party, Mr. Tibbett. Ambrose simply has to put in an appearance, but you can't imagine how thankful I was that I could truthfully say I had to stay at home until you arrived. Now, Ambrose tells me you are interested in the little dinner party we gave last week."

"I gathered from Mr. Quince," Henry said, "that it was rather more than just a party."

Rosalie's dark eyes opened wide. "What do you mean?"

Henry smiled. "I'm sure you know exactly what I mean. All the guests were people closely concerned with Lord Charlton's will, and they were brought together to be told that Simon Warwick had been found."

"Can we be sure that he was found, Mr. Tibbett?"

"Yes," said Henry. "I think we can be sure. I spent the afternoon reading your husband's file on the subject. I don't think there can be any possible doubt that Simon Finch was Simon Warwick."

"Oh, I grant you that," said Rosalie Quince, with a quick smile. "But do we know that this poor young man who was killed was really Simon Finch? You must admit the evidence is pretty scanty."

Henry said, "You have a very acute mind, Mrs. Quince—but I'm investigating a murder, not an inheritance case. I think we must assume that the man was killed because somebody thought that he was Simon Warwick. He was not a known criminal—I've checked with the Criminal Records Office. He carried the most convincing proof that he was Simon Warwick— and that fact provides the only known motive for his murder. So, until I find a better one, that's the assumption I'm going on. If, later on, it turns out that he wasn't Simon Warwick after all —well, that would be outside my terms of reference."

Rosalie frowned again. "Yes, I see what you mean. All the

people at that dinner party had some sort of interest in having the old will restored."

"Can you tell me about them, Mrs. Quince?"

"Of course. Here's a list of names and addresses. You can see that it wasn't a big dinner."

Henry glanced quickly through the list, and then said, "I'd be grateful for a little background on these people."

"I'll be glad to give it, Chief Superintendent," said Rosalie. She leaned back in her chair and took a sip of sherry. "Let's start with the Crumbles. Percy and Diana. Percy is managing director of Warwick Industries. Worked his way up from the bottom in true free-enterprise, do-it-yourself style. He started as a rough diamond, and now he's become a sharp one. As poor old Charlton got older and lazier and more complaisant, Crumble weaseled in and got everything done the way he wanted it. I don't like Percy Crumble," added Rosalie unnecessarily.

"So what does the change in the will mean to him?" Henry asked.

Rosalie laughed shortly. "What? Everything. If Simon Warwick is found, he inherits all Lord Charlton's shares—which makes him the majority shareholder and chairman of the board. Percy Crumble goes back to being managing director—just that and no more. Under the old will, Charlton's shares are sold for the benefit of various charities, and split up into a multitude of convenient proxy votes that Crumble can easily manipulate. And if Simon Warwick turned out to be an astute young man . . . well, don't quote me, but Percy might not relish a new chairman poking his nose into all the Crumble transactions."

"Indeed," said Henry. "And his wife?"

Rosalie shrugged. "Lady Diana Crumble—in her own right, of course. Nothing to do with poor Percy's little knighthood. She was born Lady Diana Gregory, Lord Ratherstone's daughter. She's not a bad old soul, even though she has a face like a horse and no sense of humor. It wasn't exactly the romantic wedding of the year. Her family needed money and Percy needed a leg up socially. Nobody else rich wanted to marry Diana, and nobody else socially prominent would have looked twice at Percy. Marriages may be made in heaven, but what was made here below was horse-trading."

Henry looked sharply at Rosalie. She was sitting engulfed in a big armchair, her legs tucked up under her, gazing into the fire. He said, "What about the Hamstones? I believe Bertram Hamstone is

73

the other executor of the will, isn't he?"

Rosalie seemed to come out of a reverie. She said, "Yes, that's right. Well, I think you can cross them off your list, because an executor doesn't stand to gain or lose either way, whatever happens to the will. Bertie's with Sprott's, you know. The private bank. Elizabeth is a nice enough old thing. Bertie's only interest could be if Sprott's and the charities had somehow . . . but that's ridiculous. I mean, Sprott's is an institution, isn't it? Now, Cecily Smeed is a different proposition altogether."

"What do you mean by that, Mrs. Quince?"

"Well, Cecily is a spinster of a certain age—she was old Charlton's secretary absolutely forever. Ambrose said the other evening that it was over thirty years. I suppose she knows more about Warwick Industries than anybody else alive. Come to think of it," Rosalie added, "she might even know something about the adoption of Simon Warwick. She was around back in those days. Anyhow, Ambrose has told me that in the original will she was left two hundred thousand pounds."

Henry nodded. "That's right. I've seen the will."

"In the new will," said Rosalie, "she gets old Charlton's inkwell and a word of thanks. Ambrose did try to get Charlton to leave Cecily's legacy intact, but the old man was absolutely fanatic— Simon must get everything. Ambrose says if Charlton had lived a bit longer, he thinks he might have talked him into reinstating Cecily. But as it is—well, I don't suppose she thinks much of an inkwell as a reward for a whole lifetime of service. I wouldn't, would you?"

"I can understand her being disappointed," said Henry. "Now, who's the last one—Mr. Denton Westbury?"

"Oh, poor Denton—he's such a sweetie. Not very bright really, but terribly nice and amusing and useful as an odd man at dinner parties."

"He's not married, then?"

Rosalie gave a little arpeggio of laughter. "Denton? Heavens, no. He lives with some little Cockney boy—a musician, I think, plays an oboe or something in a band. Of course, Denton never takes him anywhere, and nobody is supposed to know, but everybody does. The trouble is, it's difficult for a nice person like Denton to find a good job, especially as he really has no qualifications, except that he knows a whole lot of people."

"Yes, I can imagine that," said Henry.

"Well, Ambrose had the bright idea of getting Denton to run the

Charlton Foundation, which was to administer the charity funds. Of course, Ambrose and Bertie would have done the real financial work—but you see, Denton knows all the right people on the right committees, and he really does know the deserving and well-run charities from the phonies. It seemed the perfect niche for him. Poor darling Denton. He was very brave the other night, but I could see how upset he was. Anyhow, he's a realist. He's looking for another job already."

"He is?"

"Yes. It was in the personal column this morning. 'Experienced fund raiser seeks position with prominent charity'—something like that. Here, I'll show you . . . Oh, bother, it's not there. Never mind. As soon as I read it, I said to myself, 'That's Denton, all right. Good luck, boy.' "

Henry said, "Let me get this straight, Mrs. Quince. I thought that under Lord Charlton's original will, certain charities were to get certain specific bequests—"

"Well, no, not exactly. The idea was that Lord Charlton's shares in Warwick Industries were to be sold, and this big trust fund set up, which Ambrose and Bertie would administer. Lord Charlton had approved a list of charities which might apply to the fund for help. It would then be up to Denton to advise Ambrose and Bertie on the allocation of the money. Or it would have been, I should say. Or perhaps—well, if the man who was killed really was Simon Warwick, then the Charlton Foundation will go ahead, won't it. I hadn't thought of that."

"Somebody had, Mrs. Quince," said Henry. "Well, thank you very much for the sherry—and the information. Tell your husband I'll be in touch."

It was half-past seven when Henry got back to his office at Scotland Yard. He telephoned Emmy, saying that he would be home as soon as he could manage it, and then picked up the carefully worded report of Inspector Derek Reynolds's visit to Westbourne. Reynolds had been disappointed not to be able to convey his impressions in person, but his skepticism came loud and clear through the official language of the report. It ended with the information that the body had been formally identified by Mrs. Mary Busby, the deceased's landlady, as being that of her lodger, Mr. Simon Finch.

Reading it, Henry felt a quickening of excitement and interest. He had been taking it for granted that Simon Finch was Simon

Warwick—the documentary evidence seemed overwhelming. He had also—he now admitted to himself—been very close to taking it for granted that Harold Benson, Jr., had killed his rival claimant to the Charlton fortune. The mysterious American who had telephoned both Susan Benedict and Mrs. Busby bore out the theory. And yet . . . it was too neat, almost contrived. Harold Benson might well prove to be guilty in the end, but Henry was beginning to feel that he was being led by the nose down a broad, inviting trail. Too broad and too inviting.

On one point he would be able to reassure Inspector Reynolds in the morning. The man who called himself Simon Finch was no petty criminal, as Reynolds had presumed. The Criminal Records Office had no trace of his name, and a painstaking search through the files of photographs by Reynolds's assistant, Sergeant Hawthorn, had failed to turn up a face that corresponded to Ambrose Quince's picture of Simon Finch.

So the man was not a known criminal. This did not mean that he was Simon Warwick—or even Simon Finch. Identification by a landlady with whom he had lodged only for a matter of weeks was virtually worthless. Henry found himself agreeing with Inspector Reynolds's conclusion that Simon Finch might well have been an identity only recently assumed by the murder victim.

On the other hand, if the dead man was neither Finch nor Warwick, how could he have assembled all that documentary evidence? How did he come to know so much about Finch's childhood in the United States, so that his story tallied exactly with that of Mr. Bernard Grady? The only point of contact for Simon Warwick in England would seem to have been the long-closed office of Mr. Alfred Humberton, solicitor.

Simon Finch had lived in Westbourne. Humberton had practiced in Marstone. Both on the south coast. Any connection? Henry found a map of southern England, and pored over it. The two towns were nearly two hundred miles apart—Marstone being near Dover at the eastern tip of Kent, and Westbourne beyond the Solent, at the western extremity of Hampshire. No obvious link there.

Ah well, Henry thought. I'll get Reynolds to follow up whatever traces he can find of Alfred Humberton. Not that it'll be easy, after so many years. Meanwhile, Henry foresaw a busy day coming up. He took the elevator down to the garage, and drove himself through the biting rain to Chelsea, his small, old-fashioned apartment, and Emmy.

8

Next morning, Henry drove through chilly, Sunday-quiet London streets to the old-fashioned block of flats in Kensington where Miss Cecily Smeed lived. The building had a refreshing Edwardian spaciousness: its lofty ceilings and broad, carpeted stairs with curly brass rails belonged to an era when housing space in England's capital city allowed comfortable elbowroom to those who could afford it. Henry was surprised that Dumbarton Court had not already been bulldozed to make way for an efficient modern structure that would have accommodated twice as many families on the same square-footage.

The elevator was an elaborate affair of gilt and wrought iron, complete with two small chairs for those delicately nurtured passengers who could not be expected to stand. It rose with majestic slowness to the top floor—the fourth—where a neat brass plate indicated that one of the two apartments was occupied by Miss Cecily Smeed. Henry pressed the bell, hoping he was not getting Miss Smeed out of bed. It was, after all, only nine o'clock on a Sunday morning.

After a short delay, however, the door was opened by Miss Smeed, dressed in a heather-mixture tweed skirt and a cashmere sweater. Her gray hair and discreet makeup were impeccable. She looked at Henry with some surprise and no pleasure, and said,

"Good morning. What can I do for you?"

Henry introduced himself, showed his official identity card, and asked if he might come in and ask Miss Smeed a few questions. Cecily did not bat an eyelid. She simply said, "I'm afraid it is not convenient, Chief Superintendent. I have a visitor."

"This won't take long, Miss Smeed," Henry assured her. "And it is urgent. I'm afraid—"

From somewhere inside the apartment, a man's voice called, "Who is it, Cecily?"

Over her shoulder, Cecily Smeed said, "It's a detective, Denton. From Scotland Yard."

"Oh, my goodness." The voice sounded alarmed. "Is it about—?"

"I don't know what it's about," said Cecily, rather too quickly. "I have told him it is inconvenient to speak to him at the moment."

Henry said, "Is your visitor by any chance Mr. Denton Westbury, Miss Smeed?"

"It's no business of yours, but as a matter of fact—yes. And now—"

Henry beamed. "What a piece of luck," he said. "I was intending to call on him after I left you. Now I can talk to you both together. So if you don't mind—"

With a bad grace, Cecily Smeed admitted Henry to the apartment and ushered him into a drawing room into which a couple of entire modern flats would have fitted comfortably. A big bay window looked out over a panorama of rooftops to the distant dome of Saint Paul's Cathedral, and a Steinway grand piano took up no more than a corner of the space available. On a low marble table in front of the brocaded sofa, two delicate Wedgwood china cups steamed with newly made coffee. Behind the sofa, looking very much on the defensive, stood a young man with a thin, pale face and neatly trimmed sandy hair. He was dressed in brown corduroy slacks and a turtleneck pullover several sizes too large for him.

Cecily said, "This is Chief Superintendent Tibbett of Scotland Yard, Denton. Apparently he wants to talk to you."

"To me?"

"To both of you," said Henry. "How do you do, Mr. Westbury?"

"What's all this about?" Denton Westbury demanded, addressing Cecily.

She shrugged. "I have no idea," she said. "Please sit down, both of you, and I'll bring another cup of coffee."

When Cecily had gone, Henry took off his overcoat, hung it over a chair, and sat down on the sofa. Westbury remained standing. Again he said, "What on earth is all this?"

Henry said, "You may not have heard that Simon Finch was murdered yesterday."

There was a long pause. At last, Westbury said, "Yes. I had heard."

"In Ambrose Quince's office," Henry added.

"I know. Ambrose telephoned me. That's why—" He stopped.

Henry smiled. "That's why you came to see Miss Smeed. You are both affected by the death of Simon Finch—or perhaps I should say, Simon Warwick."

Cecily Smeed came back into the drawing room, carrying a third cup of coffee. Briskly, she said, "So, it's about the young man who was killed. Well, I don't see how Denton or I can possibly help you, Mr. Tibbett. I never even met Mr. Finch."

"Nor did I," said Denton Westbury, quickly.

"And yet," Henry pointed out, "when you heard the news, you came round to see Miss Smeed before nine on Sunday morning. Why?"

Before Westbury could answer, Cecily said, "Denton thought I might not have heard the news. He was quite right—Ambrose Quince didn't bother to telephone me. Naturally, Denton knew I would be interested. Of course, you must know all about Lord Charlton's will." Her eyes went for a moment to a silver-framed photograph on the piano. It showed a man in his sixties with a vigorous, aggressive face. Across the bottom, in bold handwriting, it was inscribed, "To Cecily, with gratitude—Alexander Charlton."

"Yes," said Henry. "I know about the will. About both wills, in fact. Both you and Mr. Westbury have a lot to gain from Simon Warwick's death."

Cecily said, "The dead man is Simon Finch, Mr. Tibbett. It has yet to be proved that he was Simon Warwick. For all we know, the other claimant may turn out to be Warwick after all. Or perhaps they are both fakes, and the real Simon Warwick will turn up. Ambrose Quince has three years from the date of Lord Charlton's death to trace the young man, you know."

Henry said, "Ambrose Quince is convinced that he had found Lord Charlton's nephew. As he told you, he has overwhelming proof, which he intends to lay before the courts."

Westbury began, "How do you know—?"

Henry said, "I intend to talk to everybody who was at the Quinces' dinner party last week. Apart from Mr. and Mrs. Quince, you people are the only ones who knew that Simon Warwick had been found, who knew the claimant's name, and—very importantly—who knew that he was due in Mr. Quince's office at ten o'clock yesterday morning. Also, you all stood to gain from a reversion to the old will."

Denton Westbury clutched the back of the sofa, and looked as if he might faint. He said, "But . . . Ambrose said . . . it must have been the other man . . ."

Reassuringly, Henry said, "Please understand me, Mr. Westbury—I'm not making any accusations against anybody. It's just that, for your own sakes, I must be sure that everybody who was at that party is completely in the clear. Surely you see that?"

Cecily gave an impatient little sigh. "I suppose so," she said, "but it's so foolish. You talk as though we all had motives for murder. Well, in my case, that's ridiculous."

"Two hundred thousand pounds, Miss Smeed? As opposed to an inkwell?"

Cecily said, "I am not a poor woman, Chief Superintendent. Lord Charlton made sure that I would be able to retire on a handsome pension when he—" She paused. "When he no longer needed my services. Apart from that, I have taken another job. Retirement doesn't interest me, and I have very wide experience in the business and financial world. I had no difficulty whatsoever in finding work. I am currently employed as personal assistant to Sir William Telford, the managing director of Amalgamated Textiles. Of course I would like to have two hundred thousand pounds— who wouldn't? But I can assure you that I wouldn't murder anybody to get it."

"I'm sure you wouldn't, Miss Smeed," said Henry. "Now, in Mr. Westbury's case—"

Again, Cecily answered for Westbury. "If you knew anything about London society, Mr. Tibbett, you would know that Denton is greatly in demand for organizing charitable work. Isn't that so, Denton?"

Westbury, who seemed to be feeling a little better, smiled weakly and said, "I certainly mustn't complain. I'm kept very busy. I have the contacts, you see."

"Nevertheless," Henry said, "the job with the Charlton Foundation—"

"Just a job, Mr. Tibbett. As Cecily says, I don't need it. Goodness me, no. It'll be quite a relief to be shot of it. Give me time for
other things."

Henry remembered his conversation with Rosalie Quince. He
said, "You're not looking for another job, then?"

Denton laughed, a little shrilly. "Me? Certainly not. I have more
on my plate than I can handle as it is, thank you very much."

Carefully hiding his disbelief, Henry said, "Well, that seems to
dispose of motive for both of you. Still, I'd better just get from each
of you an account of where you were yesterday morning between
nine and ten o'clock."

Westbury said quickly, "That's easy. I was at my karate class."

Showing no particular interest in the remark, Henry said, "I see.
Where is that held, Mr. Westbury?"

"The gymnasium's in High Holborn." He gave an address,
which Henry wrote down. "You can ask them. John—that's my
friend—John and I go every Saturday morning. Nine to nine-
thirty."

Henry made a note. "And after the karate class?"

There was a tiny hestitation, and then Denton said, "I came
here. To see Cecily."

"To see Miss Smeed?" Henry was surprised.

Westbury was on the defensive at once. "Any objections, Mr.
Tibbett? It just so happens that I am helping Lady Bolchester
organize a charity ball for the Distressed Gentlefolk Fund, and we
want to get Lady Telford to sit on the committee. Not that she'll be
the faintest use, of course, but if we can get Barbara Telford, then
Sir William will obviously have to cough up a decent subscription.
Now, as I told you, I have the *contacts*. Annie Bolchester was
simply going to write to Barbara, but I said to her, I said, 'That's
not the way to go about it, dear. You let me talk to Cecily Smeed.
Barbara Telford is terrified of Cecily'—sorry, Cecily dear, but it's
true, isn't it?—'and if Cecily makes a point of it—'"

Henry cut short the flow. "So you came straight here from High
Holborn. In a taxi?"

"Bus," said Westbury.

"Presumably Miss Smeed can confirm this?" Henry looked
inquiringly at Cecily, who nodded.

"Denton got here about a quarter to ten," she said, "and stayed
until about half-past."

"And you yourself, Miss Smeed?"

Cecily looked puzzled. "I was here with him, of course."

"But earlier in the morning—"

"I was having breakfast. I am not in the habit of rushing out early on Saturday morning, especially if I have an appointment."

"You were expecting Mr. Westbury, then?"

"Of course. He telephoned me on Friday evening."

Henry said, "You didn't talk to anybody—the charlady, the postman—?"

Evenly, Cecily said, "If you mean, have I an alibi, the answer is no. It would be very surprising if I did." She thought for a moment, and then said, "Anyhow, why are you interested in nine to nine-thirty? I thought Finch's appointment with Ambrose was for ten o'clock."

Vaguely, Henry said, "Oh, he turned up early for it."

"Well, then." Cecily was triumphant. "How could I possibly have known he would do that?"

"No," said Henry. "You couldn't have known, could you? Silly of me. By the way, are you going to use your influence with Lady Telford?"

"Yes, I am. If it will help Denton."

"You haven't mentioned it to her yet?"

"Of course not. I shall speak to Sir William at the office tomorrow."

Henry made a final note, and then said, "Well, I think that's all. I may have to ask you both to make formal statements later on, but I hope it won't be necessary."

"I should hope not," said Westbury, who seemed a lot chirpier. "After all, it was the Benson man who did it, wasn't it? I mean, it stands to reason. Why don't you arrest him?"

"All in good time, Mr. Westbury," said Henry with a smile. He turned to Cecily. "Just one more question, Miss Smeed. I believe you were already working for Lord Charlton when the adoption of young Simon Warwick was arranged."

Cecily raised her eyebrows. "Who told you that?"

"Mrs. Quince mentioned it." Cecily's sardonic smile deepened. "I suppose," Henry added, "that she must have heard it from her husband."

"Ambrose Quince," said Cecily, no longer smiling, "is by no means as clever as he thinks he is. If he had not been his father's son . . . well, never mind. Yes, in the technical sense, I was working for Mr. Alexander. I was sixteen years old, and a junior clerk in the outer office."

"It must have been a small organization in those days," Henry said.

"Very small, Mr. Tibbett. The mill itself was not a large concern. It was up in the Midlands, of course. We were turning out army uniforms under government contract. But Mr. Alexander was already experimenting with synthetics, and in 1944 he opened the London office. There was just himself, and his secretary Miss Harkness—she left in 1947 to get married—and Mr. Crumble, whom he brought down from the Wolverhampton plant. And myself. We started Warwick Industries—just the four of us." There was wistful remembrance mixed with pride in her voice.

"I thought Mr. Dominic Warwick—"

"Just the four of us," Cecily repeated, firmly.

"Well you must surely have heard something about the adoption at the time?"

Cecily shook her head. "I told you, I was sixteen and the office tweeny. I remember the buzz bombs, of course. And I remember the day we heard Mr. Dominic and his wife and baby had been killed." She added, "Mr. Dominic started out as a partner in the business, it's quite true, but when he got married in 1943 he sold his shares back to Mr. Alexander. He didn't care about the future."

"As it turned out, he didn't have a future, did he?" said Henry.

Sharply, Cecily said, "He wasn't to know that. He just didn't care."

Henry said, "Later on, when you became Alexander Warwick's private secretary, did he never talk to you about his nephew?"

"Never. I assumed the baby was dead, and Mr. Alexander never mentioned him."

"Well, Miss Smeed," said Henry, "if you do remember anything about those days, please let me know. Here's my office number." He stood up and put on his coat. "Thanks for the coffee. By the way, if either of you plans to leave London within the next few days, let my office know, will you? Please don't bother to see me out . . ."

As the drawing-room door closed behind him, Henry heard Denton Westbury say, "Well, that was good for a laugh."

To which Cecily Smeed replied curtly, "I'm glad you're amused."

The front door of the Crumbles' elegant house in Down Street, Mayfair, was opened by a butler, no less, who informed Henry disdainfully that Sir Percy and Lady Diana were in Scotland for the weekend. When pressed for further details, he reluctantly agreed to fetch Lady Diana's social secretary. He retreated, leaving Henry standing on the doorstep. A couple of minutes later he returned with an equally supercilious blonde who deigned to inform Henry that Sir Percy would be flying back in his private aircraft tomorrow morning and would go straight to his office from Gatwick Airport. Lady Diana, however, would be staying on at Abercrombie Castle for a few more days. Her whole tone implied that Henry should have used the tradesmen's entrance in the mews behind the house.

Henry thanked her politely, and returned to his office at Scotland Yard. A telephone call to Bertram Hamstone's house in Saint John's Wood was answered by a maid, who was ever so sorry but Mr. and Mrs. Hamstone were at their country cottage in Surrey for the weekend. They should be back late tonight. Yes, she did know the address. The house was called The Hollyhocks, and it was at Tenley Green, near Guildford.

Henry's next call was to the car pool, to request an unchauffeured car. Then he rang Emmy to tell her he would not be home to lunch, and finally pressed the buzzer that brought Sergeant Hawthorn into his office.

Tom Hawthorn was a young man with a round, fresh-complexioned face and an endearing air of perpetual eagerness, like a puppy straining at the leash. Henry had first made his acquaintance on a case in Hampshire, when Hawthorn was still a constable in the uniformed branch, and had subsequently used his good offices to get the young man transferred to the CID. Amply justifying Henry's confidence in him, Hawthorn had quickly risen to the rank of sergeant, and—since Derek Reynolds's deserved and overdue promotion to inspector—Henry had selected him to be his personal assistant. Hawthorn, for his part, regarded Henry with what the latter felt was a rather too doglike reverence and admiration, but in all other respects was shaping up nicely. Now, he stood rigidly to attention on the far side of Henry's desk, quivering with the desire to please.

"Yes, sir?"

"You've read my notes on the Finch case, Sergeant?"

"Yes, sir. Of course."

"I've just spoken to Miss Cecily Smeed and Mr. Denton Westbury. Get your notebook and sit down. I didn't take formal statements from either of them, but I want at least a record of my recollections of what was said."

Leaning back in his chair, eyes half closed, Henry dictated a précis of his recent interview, not omitting the subjects' final words.

When he had finished, Hawthorn said, "I'll go and type this up, shall I, sir?"

"No," said Henry. "Leave it with the typing pool. You and I are taking a trip to the country."

"The country, sir?"

"Tenley Green, near Guildford. We're going to talk to Mr. and Mrs. Bertram Hamstone."

Tenley Green was a pretty village far enough off the beaten track to have survived its comparative closeness to London. Mellow red-brick houses clustered round a triangular village green, complete with pond and horse trough. As Henry braked to a stop, the doors of the ancient gray stone church opened, and the congregation began straggling out into the grassy churchyard and down the path to the lych-gate—tweedy men and women turning up coat collars and knotting scarves against the chill January air, exchanging village gossip and remarks about the weather to the accompaniment of inexpert organ music from inside the church.

Henry got out of the car and went up to a large, red-faced man, who was dressed in prickly tweeds, a British Warm overcoat, and porkpie hat.

"Excuse me, sir, I wonder if you could tell me where to find a house called Hollyhocks?"

The man looked surprised and exchanged a quick glance with his companion—a thin middle-aged woman with a beaky nose. "Hollyhocks? What business do you have there, may I ask?"

Henry said, "I've come down from London to see Mr. and Mrs. Bertram Hamstone."

"You have?" Unexpectedly, the man gave a sharp roar of laughter, and the woman smiled apologetically. "Well, sir, you're looking at them now. May one ask the nature of your business? I don't think we have met."

"No, we haven't, Mr. Hamstone," Henry agreed. He took out his official identity card. "Chief Superintendent Tibbett, CID. If we might—"

"Good heavens, d'you mean Scotland Yard?" Bertram Hamstone had a penetrating voice, and several people turned and looked inquiringly. "So the crime wave has hit Tenley Green at last, has it? Well, well, well. Got a car?"

"Right there," Henry said.

"Then you'd better follow me. Mine is the yellow Mercedes."

Hamstone took his wife's arm and strode off toward a very elegant automobile parked alongside the horse trough. Henry, under the concentrated gaze of Tenley Green's population, climbed back in beside Sergeant Hawthorn and restarted his engine. Soon he was tailing the Mercedes as it wound out of the village and down a narrow lane between steep banks and trees, which reached out from either side to form a natural cloister. After a couple of miles, the Mercedes began flashing its right-hand signal, and Hamstone turned around in the driver's seat to make sure that Henry was close behind him. With a chubby forefinger he jabbed toward his right, underlining the message of the turn signal; then the car turned right and abruptly disappeared, as though swallowed up into the landscape.

Henry slowed down, and realized the reason for Hamstone's emphasis. Even had he been looking out for it, he might easily have missed the small, unmarked dirt track that turned off the tarred road and immediately lost itself in a series of tight bends among overshadowing trees. After a few hundred yards, however, the last bend suddenly brought the car out into a big circular parking area in front of a house that only a private banker could possibly have described as a cottage. It was a small Elizabethan farmhouse, red-brick and half-timbered, with a newly thatched roof and diamond-leaded windows. It had been immaculately restored, and was surrounded by a small, well-tended flower garden. Smoke rose from tall red-brick chimneys, and broad stone steps led up to a terrace that ran the length of the building.

As Hamstone climbed out of his car, the oaken front door was opened from inside, and two golden retrievers came tumbling out, tails thrashing in welcome. Elizabeth Hamstone patted the leaping dogs as introductions were made, and then Bertram Hamstone said, "Come inside and have a glass of sherry. Can't offer you lunch, I'm afraid, but you'll get a very decent meal at the Fox and Pheasant down in the village. Down, Miranda! Down, Major! I suppose you're here over this Finch affair . . ."

In the drawing room, a log fire blazed in a vast stone fireplace. Henry and Sergeant Hawthorn refused drinks. Hamstone poured himself a generous measure of pale sherry and stood with his back to the fire, legs astraddle. Elizabeth had disappeared into the recesses of the house.

Hamstone said, "Bad business, this. No doubt that the young man was murdered, I suppose?"

"None at all, I'm afraid," said Henry.

"So I gathered from Quince. Curious thing to do, wasn't it?"

Henry said, "How do you mean, curious?"

"Well, somebody wants to get the fellow out of the way—that's understandable. But an obvious murder, right there in Ambrose Quince's waiting room . . . well, I'm no expert, but I should have thought there'd have been subtler ways of disposing of Simon Warwick." Hamstone noticed Henry's look of interrogation, and gave a robust laugh. "Oh, I don't mean more sophisticated means of murder, Chief Superintendent. I mean legal ways."

"What sort of legal ways, Mr. Hamstone? I've read the file—"

Bertie Hamstone snorted. "So have, I," he said, "and I can tell you that Ambrose is by no means on to a sure thing. The evidence is pretty convincing at first glance, I'll give you that, and if there was nobody contesting the suit, I daresay a court would concur."

Henry said, "You mean—people are going to contest the fact that Simon Finch was Simon Warwick?"

Hamstone chuckled. "Not anymore, sir. Not anymore."

Enlightenment dawned on Henry. He said, slowly, "You mean that a person who wished the old will to be reinstated would have contested the claim of a live Simon Finch, to prevent him from inheriting. But once Simon Finch is dead, it's to everybody's advantage to prove that he really was Simon Warwick."

"Of course," said Hamstone. "Obvious, isn't it? The only living person who now has any interest in disproving Finch's claim is—Simon Warwick."

"So if Harold Benson should turn out to be the real Simon Warwick, he'd be the last person to want his rival dead."

Hamstone nodded approvingly. "Quite right. I see you take my point, Chief Superintendent. Benson could have challenged a live Simon Finch in the courts, and would have had the backing of a whole lot of people who were equally anxious to dispose of Finch's claim. If he now challenges a dead Simon Finch, he'll not only be one man against the world, but he'll be creating a very bad climate of public opinion against him, if he should be accused of murdering Finch."

Henry said, slowly, "He may not have thought of that."

"I never met the young man myself," said Hamstone, "only heard about him from Ambrose. I suppose if he teaches at a university he can't be a complete idiot, although one never knows these days."

Henry, feeling that he was being led off the track, said, "I daresay we'll soon know a lot more about Harold Benson, Mr. Hamstone. Meanwhile, I'm afraid I have to ask you to tell me where you and Mrs. Hamstone were yesterday morning between nine and ten o'clock. It's for your own protection, you understand."

Hamstone gave Henry an unfriendly look. "I'm not at all sure that I do understand," he said, "but the answer is very simple. Elizabeth was here—Martin drove her down on Friday evening, and you can be sure there's no shortage of witnesses to that, because there was some sort of village do—bingo evening for the Animal Welfare Fund, or some such thing. As for me—well, I don't mind admitting that that sort of affair is not my cup of tea, so I pleaded a business dinner in London and drove myself down in the Mercedes yesterday morning. I left the London house at around half-past eight—the housekeeper will be able to tell you—and got here soon after eleven."

Henry said, "Two and a half hours? We made better time than that, didn't we, Sergeant Hawthorn?"

Hawthorn said, with the trace of a grin, "Hour and forty minutes, sir."

"Good God, man, don't you know the difference between Saturday and Sunday?" Hamstone sounded rattled. "Ever tried getting out through Putney High Street on Saturday morning? Traffic's solid from the World's End to Wimbledon Common. Sunday is an entirely different matter."

"Yes, of course it is," said Henry soothingly, which provoked a sharp and suspicious look from Hamstone. He went on. "By the way, Mr. Hamstone, I understand you employ a lot of Americans in your office."

"A lot of Americans? In my office?"

"Well, in Sprott's Bank."

"Yes, there's a handful of young Americans in our organization, but none in my personal office. Why do you ask?"

"Somebody," Henry said, "telephoned Ambrose Quince's secretary on Thursday, purporting to speak from your office, and asked for Simon Finch's telephone number in Westbourne. Later on Thursday, somebody else called that number, spoke to Mr. Finch's landlady, and left a message that Mr. Quince had altered the time of Mr. Finch's appointment on Saturday from ten to nine-thirty. Mr. Quince, of course, never authorized such a call. In each case, the caller was a man with an American accent."

Very definitely, Hamstone said, "That call was not made from my office, Mr. Tibbett. I told you, I have no Americans on my immediate staff, and I would have had no possible interest in Mr. Finch's telephone number. I was especially careful not to meet either of the claimants personally. That side of the matter was entirely up to Ambrose." He paused, and then said, "Benson, one presumes?"

"One doesn't presume anything at this stage," said Henry. "Well, I think that's all for the moment, Mr. Hamstone. We'll be on our way to the Fox and Pheasant." He stood up.

Hamstone said, "Keep in touch, won't you, Chief Superintendent? Naturally, this whole affair has complicated matters concerning Lord Charlton's will. Ambrose is anxious to press ahead with court proceedings to ratify Finch's claim, but . . . well, it would be easier to do if the murder was cleared up."

"We'll do our best, Mr. Hamstone," Henry assured him, and Hawthorn nodded his earnest agreement.

In the Fox and Pheasant, Henry and Tom Hawthorn split forces, Henry making his way into the saloon bar while Tom headed for the public. The pub was crowded with the usual Sunday-morning post-Matins drinkers, and gossipy information was easy to come by. By the time that Henry and Tom foregathered in the dining room for lunch half an hour later, they were able to compare notes and reach some conclusions.

Tom Hawthorn had managed to get into conversation with Dick Martin, the Hamstones' chauffeur, who without doubt had driven Mrs. Hamstone to Tenley Green in the Rolls on Friday afternoon. Henry had overheard a large lady in a mink jacket criticize the ineffectual way in which Elizabeth Hamstone had distributed the prizes at the end of the bingo evening. Martin had complained of the way Mrs. Hamstone had tried to make him help her in the garden on Saturday morning, when he should have been cleaning the Rolls ("She think I'm a ruddy plowboy or somethink?"); while a thin lady in a beaver coat had remarked in the saloon bar that Bertie Hamstone was going to get himself into hot water with the local magistrates if he persisted in driving that frightful, vulgar yellow car of his through the village at sixty miles an hour, like he did yesterday morning. He might kill a chicken or so and get away with it by paying compensation, but one day it would be a child, or even a dog . . .

By and large, Henry and Hawthorn agreed over their excellent lunch of pork pie and cheese, local evidence confirmed the Hamstones' stories. On the other hand, there were the gaps and the small inconsistencies. .

Driving back to London, Henry gave Hawthorn his work schedule for Monday. He was to find out as much as possible about the previous lives and careers of Mr. and Mrs. Hamstone and Mr. Denton Westbury. Miss Cecily Smeed's life story, as Henry well knew, was firmly rooted in Warwick Industries, and he himself intended to visit Warwick House first thing in the morning. He planned to call on Sir Percy Crumble in his office just as soon as possible after the private jet had ferried that captain of industry from Scotland to Gatwick Airport.

Back in the comfortable, untidy apartment in Chelsea where the Tibbetts lived, Emmy was curled up on a sofa drinking a cup of tea and reading a Sunday newspaper. She got up with a pleased smile as Henry came in.

"Good, darling. You're back sooner than I expected. All through for today?"

"I hope so, Any more tea in the pot?"

"Half a moment. I'll put in some more hot water and get you a cup."

Emmy disappeared into the kitchen, and Henry picked up the paper. On the front page, but tucked into a corner, was the headline MURDER IN CITY SOLICITOR'S OFFICE, will beneath it a blurred but recognizable reproduction of the photograph of Simon Finch that Ambrose had had taken to assist him in his United States inquiries. The story under the picture was suitably vague. The victim was described as Mr. Simon Finch of Westbourne. There was no mention of Simon Warwick.

Emmy came back with a cup of tea. She said, "There's a telephone message for you. Derek Reynolds called from the Yard. Apparently he took the call, but the lady wouldn't speak to anybody but you."

"Lady?"

Emmy consulted the notepad by the telephone. "Miss Cecily Smeed. I've got her number written down. She'd like you to call back as soon as possible."

Cecily Smeed sounded positively cordial. She had been thinking back, she said, to those old days in the 1940s, and she thought she might be able to suggest a possible line of investigation for Henry.

"Oh yes, Miss Smeed? What sort of line?"

"Percy Crumble, Mr. Tibbett. I told you that Mr. Alexander had brought him down from the mill to be his administrative assistant, after Mr. Dominic pulled out of the firm. Well, I know that Mr. Alexander was very busy himself, and he delegated a lot of things to Percy. I hadn't thought about it for more than thirty years, but when Ambrose Quince mentioned the name Humberton at that dinner party, it seemed to be vaguely familiar. Now I've been able to put two and two together. I remember Percy Crumble making several telephone calls to Mr. Humberton—somewhere on the south coast, I think—and talking rather mysteriously about 'the consignment' and 'the goods to be delivered.' I remembered asking him about it—I said that I had no record of any customer of that name, or any consignment due, and he simply told me to shut up and mind my own business. Well, now I realize he must have been talking about the Warwick baby. You should ask him about it."

"Thank you, Miss Smeed. I'll certainly do that," Henry assured her.

9

Sir Percy Crumble's office in Warwick House, Mayfair—a well-aimed stone from Berkeley Square could have broken its window—was opulent in the extreme. Percy Crumble had apparently never heard of the one-upmanship of the super-executive who chooses to work in surroundings of Spartan simplicity: if he had, he would have considered the idea to be potty, just as he had regarded it as a sign of senility when Lord Charlton himself had refused a suite of offices in the new steel and plate-glass building, preferring to do what work he did for the company from his library in Belgrave Terrace.

Cecily Smeed, of course, had until recently occupied an office not so very inferior to Percy's at Warwick House, where she was always at Lord Charlton's disposal for confidential secretarial work. Nevertheless, memos from the old man had frequently turned up on the desks of his top executives, handwritten with an old-fashioned pen dipped into the silver inkwell that Cecily was now to inherit. These memos always caused great confusion, because they photocopied very badly, and there was no authorized distribution list for them. Cecily would only smile infuriatingly and say, "I think Lord Charlton simply meant it as a personal note to you, Sir Percy." If you asked Percy Crumble, Warwick Industries was bloody well better off without the both of them—Cecily and the old man. But, of course, one couldn't say so in public.

He received the news that Chief Superintendent Tibbett of Scotland Yard wished to see him, with some irritation but no alarm. He had read his Sunday paper in Scotland and was well aware that Ambrose Quince's candidate for Simon Warwick had been murdered in Ambrose's own office. He realized that Scotland Yard would have to make an investigation, and that Warwick Industries was bound to be a part of it. He asked his secretary—an attractive but unostentatious blonde—if he could fit Chief Superintendent Tibbett into his morning schedule.

"You could see him right away, Sir Percy. You remember, we kept this morning free in case there was any delay in your flight from Scotland."

"Okay. Send 'im in. Better get doon with it."

Like most people meeting Sir Percy Crumble for the first time, Henry was impressed that such a titan of the business world should have been able to remain so unsophisticated, so North Country, so bluff and foursquare and commonsensical. With many people—those lucky enough never to find themselves in a competitive situation with Sir Percy—this impression remained permanent. Others had to learn the hard way that Percy Crumble's provincial accent was a deliberately variable characteristic, and that his country-bumpkin façade disguised one of the sharpest minds in big business. Henry was deceived for about fifteen seconds. Then his brain took over.

"So poor yoong Finch was doon in, and in Ambrose's own office? Well, 'oo'd 'ave thought it. I suppose 'twas t'other chap did it." Crumble beamed at Henry. " 'Ave a cigar." He pushed a Venetian tooled leather box across the gleaming desk.

Declining the cigar, Henry said, "Do you personally believe that Simon Finch was Simon Warwick, Sir Percy?"

"Don't see 'ow anybody could fail to do so. Not with the evidence Ambrose collected."

"You never met the young man yourself, did you?"

"No, I didn't. Didn't 'ave a mind to. Better get the 'ole thing settled legally first, that was my feeling."

Henry said, "I believe you had something to do with the adoption, back in 1944."

Percy Crumble grinned. "So our Cecily's been talking, 'as she? Might 'ave known. Yes, I telephoned 'Umberton woonce or twice, as Mr. Alexander told me to. Just about practical details—where the baby was to be collected from, and that. Great

Ormond Street 'Ospital for Children—that's where 'e was at. My job was to get 'im from there down to 'Umberton's office in Marstone, where the adoptive parents were picking 'im up."

"You mean, you took the baby down yourself?"

"No, no, no." Sir Percy laughed. "Fine sight I'd 'ave been, with a two-week-old baby. No, foonily enough, it was Diana—that's my wife, although of course she wasn't then—it was Diana took 'im down. She being a friend of Mrs. Dominic's from school days. She was driving an ambulance in Loondon, then. Took yoong Simon down on the train on 'er day off. That was the first time I ever met 'er. After that, we lost tooch for years."

Henry said, "Did the name Finch mean anything to you, Sir Percy? I mean, did Mr. Humberton ever mention the name of the adoptive parents?"

Crumble shook his head. "Never," he said. "Captain X, it always was. And the poor kid referred to as 'the consignment of goods.' More like a ruddy smuggling than a regular adoption, as I said to Mr. Alexander at the time."

"You did? What was his reaction?"

"Oh, just said that it was the way these things had to be done." Crumble's North Country accent was beginning to wane.

"Did you ever see the baby yourself, Sir Percy?"

Crumble shook his head. "He was just a bill of goods like I said, poor little bugger. But Diana saw him, all right."

"And you can both confirm that Mr. Humberton was the solicitor through whom the adoption was arranged?"

"Certainly we can."

"That would seem to clinch the case that Simon Finch was Simon Warwick."

"Like I said, Chief Superintendent, Ambrose has all the evidence he needs, and the sooner it's proved in court, the better."

"The better for you, Sir Percy?"

"The better for Warwick Industries." Sir Percy Crumble lit a cigar, and his brown eyes twinkled at Henry through the smoke as he puffed at it. "Save your breath, now. You're thinking that I had a good motive for disposing of Simon Finch, and you're asking yourself where I was on Saturday morning. And you're wondering 'ow best you can ask *me* the same question, tactfully. Well, consider it asked, and I'll tell you. The wife and I flew oop to Scotland Friday evening, to stay with Lord Abercrombie. I just got back this morning, and she's still there."

"That seems very straightforward." Henry took details of the plane, the flight number, and the times. Then he said, "You landed at Edinburgh. How did you get on from there?"

There was a little pause, and then Crumble said, "Bobby Abercrombie sent a car. It's a two-hour drive."

"So what time did you get to Abercrombie Castle?"

With no pause this time, Crumble said, "Diana must have got there about nine in the evening. I stayed in Edinburgh—had some business there. If you want to check, I saw our Scottish agent, Bill Fyfe, in his office at eleven on Saturday morning. Caught the eleven thirty-five train to Abercrombie and got to the castle in time for a late lunch."

Henry made a careful note, studied it, but said nothing. Sir Percy said, crossly, "You're not suggesting I could 'ave nipped back to Loondon and murdered this character, are you?"

With a broad smile, Henry said, "You had a private plane at your disposal and there are also the scheduled flights. I'll have to check on it. It's the sort of thing that's always being done in detective stories."

Crumble's smile matched Henry's. "Well, if you find it can be doon let me know," he said. "Might come in useful in the way of business." He stood up and extended his hand. "Nice meeting you, Chief Superintendent. Let me know 'ow things coom along. Good to get this matter settled, and know woonce and for all that Simon Warwick is dead. Then we can all go about our business."

Henry went back to his office to make up his notes and go through his "in" tray before taking lunch in the cafeteria. There seemed to be little of interest. Pathologists' reports and fingerprint analyses on the Finch case merely confirmed what was already obvious—that Simon Finch had been strangled after having been rendered unconscious by a blow to the neck such as is employed in karate or unarmed combat. Fingerprints of Ambrose Quince and Susan Benedict had been found, as expected, in the office and waiting room, with a few of Simon Finch's superimposed where one would expect to find them—on the arms of the chair in which he sat, and on the newspaper that he had been holding. Harold Benson's prints were on the arms of Finch's chair—consistent with his story of finding the body. The most significant thing, to Henry, was that there was no evidence that any surface had been wiped clean.

The only other communication said that a Mrs. Goodman had

telephoned, asking to speak to Chief Superintendent Tibbett personally. She had been told that he was out, and the call transferred to Inspector Reynolds. Henry went off with a tranquil mind to eat his lunch.

His tranquillity was shattered just as he had finished his beef stew and before he had started on the tinned peaches. Derek Reynolds loomed up beside the table, looking distinctly perturbed.

"I'm sorry to disturb your lunch, sir, but there's a lady in my office I think you should see."

Henry swallowed a spoonful of peaches, and said, "Can't it wait ten minutes?"

"It's about the Finch case, sir. I think you should see her."

Resignedly, Henry abandoned the remains of his lunch and followed Reynolds out into the corridor. Reynolds said, "It's a Mrs. Goodman, sir. Seems a respectable woman. She says—well, the fact is, she says she recognizes the photograph of Simon Finch, and that he's not Simon Finch at all. She's demanding to see the body so that she can make a positive identification."

"She seems to be very sure of herself on the basis of a smudged newspaper photograph," Henry remarked.

"If she's right," Reynolds said, "then it's hardly surprising. You see, she says she's his mother."

Mrs. Edith Goodman was standing in Inspector Reynolds's office with her back to the door, looking out the window over the gray January roofscape. She turned as Reynolds and Henry came in, and Henry was immediately struck by a strong resemblance between this woman and the man he knew as Simon Finch. Mrs. Goodman was tall, with the same long, thin features and untidy fair hair, now tinged with white. She said, "You are Chief Superintendent Tibbett?"

"That's right."

"Then please put me out of my agony, Mr. Tibbett. Let me see my son." She spoke the English of the solid, respectable middle class—the small shopkeepers, the clerks, the teachers, the civil servants, the people who quietly keep a country ticking over.

Henry said, "Do sit down, Mrs. Goodman. I think first of all you should tell me about yourself, and why you are so sure that Simon Finch is your son."

She sat down. "His name isn't Simon Finch. It's Ronald Goodman. I'm his mother, Edith, and his father was Ernest Goodman, my late husband. Ronald was born in Surbiton, where we were living then, in 1944. My husband was with the Ministry of Health. He retired in 1956 and we moved down to the south coast. My husband died in 1965, but Ronald and I went on living in the bungalow at Ketterham-on-sea."

Henry remembered the map he had been studying. He said slowly, "That's not far from Marstone, is it?"

Edith Goodman looked surprised. "Fancy you knowing Ketterham," she said. "It's such a small village, most people don't. Yes, you're right, it's only a half-hour bus ride out of Marstone, which made it convenient for Ronald's work."

Henry nodded. Things were falling into place. "His work as a solicitor's clerk. He worked for Mr. Alfred Humberton, didn't he?"

"Well, really, Mr. Tibbett," said Mrs. Goodman, "if you know all this about Ronald, how did you come to think his name was Simon Finch?"

Impetuously, Inspector Reynolds interrupted. "The typewriter, sir. I told you about the typewriter."

"Yes, yes, I know, Reynolds."

Mrs. Goodman was looking from one to the other in bewilderment. "What's all this about a typewriter?"

"Never mind for the moment, Mrs. Goodman. I'll explain later. Now, when did Ronald leave home?"

"It was three years ago. Two years after poor Mr. Humberton died and the office closed down. Ronald had worked ever so hard, you know, clearing everything up. And then he found himself out of a job. He finally got another position in Marstone, but he wasn't really happy. He wanted to better himself, you see, so he went off to London. At first he wrote regularly, but then the letters got less and less—you know what young people are like, Mr. Tibbett— until it was a year and more since I heard. I've tried to trace him, but he lived in digs and was always moving about, and nobody could help me. And then . . ." Her voice trembled, but she pulled herself together and went on steadily, "Then I saw the photograph in yesterday's paper and I knew it was my boy. I couldn't mistake him."

Henry said, "Did Ronald every marry, Mrs. Goodman?"

"Not that I know of. Certainly not up to the time he left home. And he'd have told me, and brought the girl to see me. I'm quite sure of that. It wasn't as if we had quarreled, or anything. We just drifted apart, as it were. I expect he was doing well for himself, and didn't have time for . . ." Mrs. Goodman quickly pulled a handkerchief out of her handbag and dabbed her eyes, as if ashamed of her tears.

Gently, Henry said, "I'm very sorry, Mrs. Goodman. I'm afraid you may be right, and that the poor young man may be your son. We would all be grateful if you would identify him for us."

Mrs. Goodman nodded, the handkerchief still to her eyes.

Henry went on, "The name Finch doesn't mean anything at all to you?"

The woman shook her head, emphatically. Then she looked up at Henry, and said, "Why? Why, Mr. Tibbett? Why should anybody want to kill Ronald?"

Henry sighed. "I think," he said, "it was because somebody believed he was Simon Finch."

"And why should they do that?"

"Because he said he was, Mrs. Goodman."

Mrs. Goodman bore up remarkably bravely under the ordeal of identifying the body, which she stated was undoubtedly that of her son, Ronald. She also provided Henry with the name and address of Ronald Goodman's dentist in Marstone, through whom positive dental identification could be made. She then asked, almost shyly, if she might be responsible for the funeral arrangements. Henry offered a police car to drive her to the railway station, but she replied that it was only a step to Victoria and she would rather walk. It had been rather a shock, but it was better to know the worst, wasn't it? She then left Scotland Yard with great dignity.

In Henry's office, Henry and Reynolds went over the latest development with Sergeant Hawthorn, who had come to report on his morning's work.

"Everything will have to be checked out, Sergeant," Henry said, "but personally I'm convinced that the woman's story is absolutely true. Apart from documentary evidence, the so-called Simon Finch was the unlikeliest person to be Simon Warwick. On the other hand, he was the epitome of a solicitor's clerk from Ketterham-on-sea. The family resemblance alone would have convinced me that he was Mrs. Goodman's son."

"And he worked for Alfred Humberton," said Reynolds.

"The really significant thing," said Henry, "is that he cleared out the office after the old man's death. Quince told us that all papers relating to living clients were returned to them, and 'dead' files destroyed. Obviously, young Goodman must have come across the

Warwick-Finch file, and decided it was worth keeping. And so it turned out to be. He was able to produce the original correspondence."

Tom Hawthorn, his head to one side, said, "Could I say something, sir?"

"Of course, Sergeant."

"Well, I was thinking—I mean, Humberton's file would have the carbons of Humberton's letters in it, wouldn't it, not the originals?"

Henry grinned. "Quite right. But I think Inspector Reynolds can fill in that gap."

He glanced at Reynolds, who said, "Here's how it was done. Goodman must have found and kept some old office-letterhead notepaper—not difficult to do that—*and* he kept the old office typewriter which had been used for more than twenty years for Humberton's correspondence. Once he heard the search for Simon Warwick was on, all he had to do was to retype Humberton's letters and forge a scrawl of a signature. If an analysis was made—"

"It was," Henry put in.

"Well, there you are. What was the result, sir?"

"According to Quince, the paper was shown to be at least thirty years old, and the typewriter identical with that used for other documents from Humberton's office. That seemed good enough. Now, of course, they'll start on the signatures, which will undoubtedly tell a different story."

Reynolds went on. "The landlady at Westbourne told me that Finch—Goodman, that is—had done a lot of typing when he first went to live there, before Christmas. Then he conveniently disposed of the old typewriter—threw it in the sea, I expect."

Almost admiringly, Hawthorn said, "Made a proper job of it, didn't he?"

"Rather too good a job for his own safety," said Henry, dryly. "So good that he got himself murdered."

Tentatively, Reynolds said, "I suppose he could have been murdered because of something in his own life, as Ronald Goodman."

"I very much doubt it," Henry said, "but of course we'll have to investigate that aspect of it. You'd better forget the Hamstones and Westbury, Hawthorn, and go after the late Ronald Goodman."

"Yes, sir," said Hawthorn. "I did manage to do a bit this morning, sir. It's all there."

Left alone, Henry read Hawthorn's report. It consisted merely of facts available from various public records. Bertram Hamstone had been in his first term at Oxford when the war broke out in 1939. He had at once left university and volunteered for the army, ending up as a Royal Marine Commando. During the war, in 1944, he had married Elizabeth Barrington, a hospital nurse. After the war, he had returned to Oxford, graduated, and joined Sprott's Bank. His father was Sir Albery Hamstone, now deceased, a governor of the bank. The family was extremely well-to-do. It was an unremarkable, if enviable, life story.

As for Denton Westbury, there was no birth certificate issued for anybody of that name that could be traced in the records. This, Sergeant Hawthorn pointed out, was probably because the name was a false one. This was no crime, unless the man was passing himself off as the real Denton Westbury, with intent to defraud— which was clearly not the case. He had come to London, as far as Hawthorn had been able to ascertain, about seven years ago. At that time, he had been a partner in an interior-decorating business, and had achieved some small fame in exalted circles by redecorating Lord Charlton's house in Belgrave Terrace. Despite this *succès d'estime*, however, the decorating venture had failed, and Mr. Westbury had taken to fund raising for worthy charities. He was known as a homosexual and a protégé of Miss Cecily Smeed's. It was through her, it was said, that he had obtained the commission from Lord Charlton, and it was she who had introduced him to the moneyed and aristocratic ladies who sat on committees for charity balls. A terse footnote from Hawthorn pointed out that most of this information was strictly backstairs gossip, and he could not vouch for its accuracy at this stage.

Henry read the report, then put it aside and sat for some minutes deep in thought. Then he said aloud, "Damn it, there must have been *something*."

Ambrose Quince had already left the office for the day when Henry telephoned at half-past four. Susan Benedict alibied expertly for him. "I'm so sorry, Chief Superintendent, Mr. Quince just left for a business appointment, and he'll be going straight home afterward. You should be able to get him at the Ealing number after six."

Henry rang the Ealing number right away, and was not in the least surprised to be told by Rosalie that Ambrose had been home for some time.

"He likes to get back before it's dark on these winter evenings. Hold on, I'll get him."

Ambrose Quince received Henry's news first with derision, then with disbelief and finally with dismay. "You say there's no doubt at all?"

"None whatsoever, Mr. Quince."

"But . . . my case is all ready to submit to the courts."

"Then you'd better annul it, or whatever the legal term is. What it boils down to is that Simon Finch is Simon Warwick, but that Ronald Goodman was not Simon Finch."

"I had those documents expertly analyzed, you know. Both the paper and the typewriter are identical to . . ."

Patiently, Henry explained. There was a silence. Then Ambrose said, "Well, I'll be damned." Suddenly he started to chuckle. "This'll stir up a hornet's nest. So somebody murdered the wrong man by mistake? Well, well, well. Will you tell the others, or shall I?"

Henry said, "I think you should tell your people—that is, the Hamstones, Sir Percy, Miss Smeed, and Mr. Westbury. You can leave it to me to break the news to Mr. Harold Benson."

"Good Lord, I'd almost forgotten him. Now I suppose we'll have to start looking into his claim again."

"That's entirely your affair, Mr. Quince. One thing did occur to me, though. You say that Finch—or Goodman—claimed he had been enrolled at an English school, from which he ran away. Did you check that out?"

"As far as we could," said Quince. "He gave us the name of the place, and it turned out to be a private school on the south coast somewhere, which closed down eight years ago. Not a hope in hell of tracing any records."

"He thought of everything, didn't he?" Henry said. "Meanwhile, I have to try to find out who killed him. And in that connection—I've a favor to ask you."

"A favor?"

"As Lord Charlton's executor," Henry said, "I suppose you had to go through all his papers."

"I'm still at it, old boy. Finding Simon Warwick is only a small part of what I have to cope with. I really feel Bertie Hamstone ought to help me, but what can you do with a man who spends half the week in the country and then says he's too busy to . . . Oh, well. Never mind. What do you want of me?"

Henry hesitated. Then he said, "I have a feeling that there might be . . . something relevant . . . among Lord Charlton's most personal papers. Things he would have kept at home, not in the office. In his private desk, probably."

Ambrose said, "If you'll give me an idea of the sort of thing you're looking for, I'll see what I can find."

"That's the trouble," Henry said. "I don't know what I'm looking for."

"Really, old man—" Ambrose sounded both amused and exasperated. He had formed quite a high opinion of Henry's abilities, but if this was the way that senior detectives went about their business . . .

"What I would like," said Henry, "is permission to go through Lord Charlton's personal papers myself."

This produced a predictable defensive barrage from Ambrose, who felt obliged to protect his client's privacy even after death. Only Henry's veiled but definite threat to inspect the papers with a search warrant, if he could not do so without one, finally made Ambrose agree. After all, he could see no harm in it. Just a little irregular. It was arranged that he and Henry should meet at the house on Belgrave Terrace at eleven o'clock the following morning, Tuesday.

Next, Henry telephoned the Kensington hotel where Harold Benson was staying.

"Mr. Benson? I wondered if I might come along in half an hour or so and have a word with you."

Harold Benson sounded jaunty and a little nervous. He said, "Coming to arrest me after all, Chief Superintendent?"

"Not this time," said Henry. "I've got some rather interesting news for you. I'd like to discuss it privately with you before we go to the Yard and take a formal statement."

"A formal statement?" Benson was definitely shaken.

"Witnesses have to make formal statements, you know," said Henry, soothingly. "See you in half an hour."

10

Harold Benson, Henry thought, seemed less at ease than usual. Not surprisingly, perhaps, because teatime in a Kensington hotel must always be something of an ordeal for an American. Not even the most Anglophilic Virginian matrons could have prepared Mr. Benson for the hushed chintziness, the tinkle of spoons, the discreet half-whispered conversations interspersed with shrill demands for more buttered toast, the inexorable femininity and elderliness of the occasion.

At a corner table behind a potted palm, Harold Benson looked hopelessly at the dented metal teapot and the plate of dried-up rock cakes, and suggested that Henry might officiate. Resisting a wicked impulse to confuse the young man even further by suggesting that he be mother, Henry poured out two cups of insipid tea, and said, "Well, Mr. Benson, the mystery of Simon Finch has been solved."

Benson put down his teacup with a clatter, which caused two ladies in mauve hats to suspend their conversation for long enough to give him an admonitory look. He said, "What do you mean by that, Chief Superintendent?"

Henry said, "Just that the young man who was murdered was not Simon Finch after all."

Benson seemed to relax. He leaned back in his chair and said, "Who was he?"

"His name was Ronald Goodman. He used to work in the office of the lawyer who arranged the adoption of Simon Warwick. That was how he got hold of the papers which he used to convince Mr. Quince of the soundness of his claim."

Benson smiled, apparently genuinely amused. "I knew it must have been something like that," he said. "The man was an obvious fake."

Henry said, "Ronald Goodman was a fake, Mr. Benson. Simon Finch was not."

"I'm afraid I don't—"

"I think you do, Mr. Benson. Simon Warwick was adopted by a couple named Finch who lived in McLean, Virginia. He was brought up as Simon Finch. Ronald Goodman was not Simon Finch. Are you?"

Looking rattled, Benson said, "I am Simon Warwick."

"If you are," Henry said, "then you are not Harold R. Benson, Jr. You know about that. I don't. I've come here this afternoon, quite unofficially, to warn you."

"Warn me? Of what?"

"Well," Henry said, "look at it like this. If you are really Harold Benson, putting forward a false claim to be Simon Warwick, then you run a grave risk of being arrested for fraud, and maybe also for the murder of your rival claimant. After all, you must admit that you had both motive and opportunity."

Benson opened his mouth to protest, but Henry went on. "That could let you in for a stiff prison sentence, but nothing worse. We don't have the death penalty in England."

"But—"

"On the other hand, if you are not Harold Benson, but Simon Finch—that is, Simon Warwick—then you may well pay for it with your life. Ronald Goodman was a stupid, greedy young man—nothing more—and he was killed because somebody believed that he really was Simon Finch. It was a mistake. Do you think that a person who has gone to those lengths once to eliminate Simon Warwick would hestitate to kill again, if he's convinced he's now got the right man?"

Benson was pale but firm. He said again, "I am Simon Warwick."

"Where did you get Simon Warwick's passport, Mr. Benson?"

"I told Quince. From my mother."

"From Mrs. Harold R. Benson, Sr.?"

There was a tiny hesitation before Benson replied, "Of course."

Henry stood up. He said, "Thank you for the tea, Mr. Benson. Take care of yourself. Accidents can happen, you know. If by any remote chance you really are Simon Warwick, alias Simon Finch, alias Harold Benson—then I should disprove the Benson alias right away and come to us for police protection until your case is heard and proven. Whoever went to all the trouble of murdering Ronald Goodman is going to be very cross indeed when the news breaks."

The next morning, Henry found himself in the library of Lord Charlton's Belgravia house, accompanied by Ambrose Quince. The room looked very different from the warm retreat that Ambrose remembered from his last visit to Lord Charlton. Now the furniture was shrouded in dust-sheets, the fireplace was empty and clean-swept, and the room had the chilly feeling of an unoccupied house in winter, when the heating has been adjusted to the lowest possible point that will not actually damage the furniture.

Ambrose shivered as he fumbled in his pocket for keys. He said, "I wish I knew how to turn the thermostat up. Nobody living here now, of course. The house comes up for auction next month."

Henry said, "I thought that if Simon Warwick was found, he would inherit this house."

Ambrose sneezed and blew his nose. "Blasted cold coming on," he said. "No, Bertie Hamstone and I agreed on the sale. Now that our prime claimant has turned out to be not only dead, but a phony, there's no sense in letting this good furniture rot—not to mention the house. The proceeds of the sale will go into the estate, of course. But until we find the real Simon Warwick—"

Henry said, tentatively, "Harold Benson?"

Ambrose shook his head decisively. "No chance of it."

"Young Finch ran away from home," Henry said, thinking aloud. "He took another identity. You were always convinced that the two boys knew each other. Supposing that Harold Benson is dead, and that his friend Simon Finch took over—"

Ambrose sneezed again. Tetchily, he said, "That's ridiculous. Benson's life is perfectly straightforward and documented—birth, home, school, university, and job. No, the obvious answer is that Benson knew Simon Finch and got the passport from him somehow. So Benson decides on an impersonation. He can't get away from having to use his own passport and birth certificate, but he knows enough about Finch's story to provide more or less plausible stories to cover the discrepancies."

Henry rubbed his nose with his forefinger. He said, "I wonder."

Ambrose was not listening. He went on, "And since Finch has not come forward, despite all the publicity, it's also obvious that he's not in a position to come forward—in plain words, that he's dead. We'll advertise again, of course—for Simon Finch, this time—but we'll get no genuine claimant, you mark my words. Then we'll go to court and ask for leave to presume the death of Simon Warwick, otherwise Finch. And that will be that."

Henry had walked over to the window, which looked out onto a small, damp patio with upended wrought-iron furniture. He said, "This was where you had that talk with Lord Charlton, wasn't it? In this room, I mean."

"Yes." Ambrose sounded suitably somber. "Poor old man."

"And he told you that he would recognize his nephew."

"Oh, that." Ambrose sneezed for the third time. "I didn't take that very seriously. I suppose he thought he'd be able to see a family likeness . . . he was very fond of his brother Dominic, or so my father told me. Liked his wife too, I believe. Well, now, if we can get on, because I've got a client coming at twelve . . ."

Henry said, "I really don't need to keep you here, Mr. Quince. All I need are the keys to the desk. I'll lock everything up when I'm through, and drop the keys back at your office."

"Well . . ." Ambrose was dubious.

"I won't take anything away," Henry reassured him. "Any documents that I may want to have photocopied, I'll put to one side and we can arrange for it later on."

"I suppose there's no harm in it." Ambrose allowed himself to be convinced. He snuffled his way out into a taxi, and through the streaming streets to Theobald's Road, where he allowed Miss Benedict to keep the client waiting seven minutes while he did the *Times* crossword puzzle.

In Lord Charlton's library, Henry sat at the big, old-fashioned desk, opening the drawers one by one, and feeling like a Peeping Tom. In fact, there was little that was not of a purely business or social nature. There were invitations to great houses; some old theater and opera programs, mostly for gala charity performances at huge prices; some yellowing race cards and Royal Enclosure badges. Receipts from a famous firm of jewelers for expensive items purchased at random intervals seemed to confirm what Henry's discreet inquiries had revealed about Lord Charlton's private life—that he had confined himself to a series of affairs with attractive but unremarkable ladies, each of whom was suitably rewarded before being gently dismissed. None of them, it was clear, had ever invaded the sanctum of Belgrave Terrace.

The lowest drawer of the desk was the only one that yielded any sort of human information. There was an old manila envelope containing a number of black-and-white photographs, now turning sepia from age. A family group dating from the early years of the century showed a mustachioed father and a simpering blonde mother stiffly posed with two small boys. The taller, dark boy had his hand resting protectively on the shoulder of a small, impish, fair-haired lad. On the back, in handwriting that Henry recognized as an immature version of that which he had seen in Cecily Smeed's drawing room, was written "Father, mother, Dominic and self. Christmas 1913." There were school photographs of football teams ("1st eleven, Bingham Primary School, 1919. Dominic second from left, front row"), and amateur theatricals ("Dominic as Rosalind!!! 1922"). In 1930, Dominic—a fresh-faced youth in his twenties—was photographed on the beach at Blackpool. In 1934 he was snapped standing proudly beside a boxlike saloon car. In 1938, the brothers had evidently taken a trip to Europe, for Dominic appeared gracing the foreground of the Eiffel Tower and Saint Peter's Square.

The last photograph of Dominic was his wedding picture from 1943. It had been a wartime wedding, without frills. There was no sign of any members of the older generation from either family— just a group of young adults of both sexes, mostly in uniform. Alexander Warwick, in civilian clothes, stood shoulder to shoulder with the bridegroom—the latter still recognizable as the mischievous three-year-old of the first photograph. The bride, in a square-shouldered, short-skirted suit and a perched, flowery hat, was a pretty but not memorably beautiful girl. Henry searched the pictured faces of Dominic and Mary Warwick for familiar features, but found none.

He was about to return the photographs to the envelope when he noticed that there was a piece of folded paper still in it. An old letter. Henry pulled it out and read it. It was written on the printed notepaper of the firm of Quince, Quince, Quince and Quince.

September 9, 1949

Dear Alex,

I have just got back from America, where I paid the visit which I promised you. In accordance with our agreement, I will not mention to which part of the United States my journey took me. I passed myself off to Captain and Mrs. X as a colleague of Fred Humberton's, which in a way I suppose I am.

I recognized the boy at once—he is already strikingly like his father, but with his mother's eyes. He seems in good health and spirits, and Mrs. X is a most charming woman. They appear to be comfortably off, and I don't think the boy will lack for anything material.

I know that in 1944 I advised you to adopt Simon, and you decided otherwise. Now, he is thoroughly settled in his new home, and I would advise you to put the matter out of your mind and concentrate on the things which really interest you. The moment for action has past, Alex, and you would do more harm than good by stirring things up at this stage. However, for the distant future, you might do well to remember that he is your rightful heir, and that yours is a family business.

As always,
Bobby

P.S. Judith and young Ambrose send their regards.

Henry read the letter twice, thoughtfully. So Charlton had not abandoned his nephew as definitively as he had led Ambrose Quince to believe. Five years after the adoption, he had arranged for Ambrose's father to visit the boy, and Robert Quince's letter hinted strongly that Alexander Warwick was at that time considering the possibility of getting young Simon back. In fact, the letter opened up a lot of interesting lines of thought.

Meanwhile, Henry reminded himself, fascinating as the mystery of Simon Warwick might be, his job was to investigate the murder of Ronald Goodman. Sitting in the chill discomfort of the late Lord Charlton's library, Henry considered Ronald Goodman, whom he had never known alive.

Everybody—Henry included—had taken it for granted that the young man had been killed by somebody who believed him to be Simon Warwick, and wished him out of the way. But that assumption left a lot of unanswered questions. How had Goodman found out the details of young Finch's running away from home? Had Goodman really kept the Simon Warwick correspondence and the old office typewriter all those years, just on the unlikely chance that Lord Charlton might alter his will? Wasn't it more probable that Goodman knew a lot more about Simon Warwick-Finch than just his name? Why had Simon Finch not come forward to claim his inheritance? Was it because he was dead—or was there another reason why he dared not reveal himself? A reason that Goodman knew about, perhaps. If so, who would have a stronger motive for killing Goodman that Simon Warwick himself?

Henry stood up and went to the window. Aloud, he said, "Who is Simon Warwick?" Harold Benson? Ambrose Quince . . . *Ambrose Quince?* I'm getting fanciful, Henry decided. Everybody of the right age and sex, with Mary Warwick's blue eyes, flitted tantalizingly across his mind as a possible candidate. It seemed likely that Simon Finch had come over to England when he left home, and that his adoptive mother had flown over to look for him after his father's death. Ambrose Quince's father knew that Simon Finch was Simon Warwick. Might he not have told his son?

Denton Westbury had the basic qualifications to be Simon Warwick, and it seemed certain that Westbury was an assumed name. Why was he so involved with Warwick Industries, and with Cecily Smeed, who probably knew more than she was admitting?

Suddenly, with a stirring of the instinct that Henry's colleagues called his "nose," he felt quite certain that Simon Warwick was not dead, as Ambrose Quince was now set on proving. Simon Warwick was alive, and very much aware of everything that was happening. I've almost certainly met him and spoken to him, Henry thought. There's some reason why he can't come forward under his own name. But he means to lay hands on that inheritance, one way or another. Of course he knew all along that Goodman was a phony—but a phony with a good chance of getting away with it. So Goodman had to be killed.

On that basis, it seemed to Henry most relevant to his murder investigation to establish the identity of Simon Warwick.

Back in his office at Scotland Yard, Henry had only just taken off his wet raincoat when the telephone rang.

"Reynolds here, sir. I've got Mr. Harold Benson in my office."

"You have? Why?"

"He insisted on seeing me, sir, and he wants to talk to you. He says somebody just tried to kill him."

11

The first and most obvious thing that Henry noticed about Harold Benson was that he was scared out of his wits. Gone was the jaunty, self-confident young man who had the day before asserted that he was Simon Warwick and had appeared not unduly perturbed when warned that an attempt might be made on his life. He sat in front of Henry's desk, as white as a sheet, nervously clasping and unclasping his hands. Either he's a bloody good actor, Henry thought, or he really is frightened.

Aloud, Henry said, "So you think that somebody tried to kill you, Mr. Benson?"

"I don't just think it. I know it. Damn near succeeded, too." With shaking fingers, Benson pulled a pack of cigarettes out of his pocket. "Okay if I smoke?"

"Of course."

There was a moment of silence as Benson, with some difficulty, got his cigarette lit. The he said, "In broad daylight. In the middle of Piccadilly. I couldn't believe it."

"What happened, Mr. Benson?"

Benson gave a small, nervous laugh. "It sounds crazy," he said, "but somebody tried to push me under a bus."

Henry raised his eyebrows very slightly, and Benson's pale face flushed angrily. "I suppose you don't believe me, but it's true. I left the hotel around ten o'clock this morning to do some shopping—things my wife wants me to bring back from England. Anyone could have followed me. I took a bus to Piccadilly, and I was waiting with a whole crowd of people to cross the street to Fortnum and Mason's when it happened. The lights had just turned green for the traffic, and those huge buses were coming down the bus lane at a good rate. I was on the edge of the curb, and somebody pushed me from behind. Hard. I stumbled off the curb, and how I kept my footing, I don't know. That bus driver was some guy. He jammed on his breaks and missed me by inches. Stuck his head out of the cab and called me a few rude names, too. By that time, the lights had changed and all the other people were across the street."

"You didn't recognize anybody in the crowd?"

"How could I? Anyway, who do I know in London apart from Quince and his secretary? I certainly didn't see either of them."

"Look here, Mr. Benson," Henry said, reasonably, "don't you think you may be taking this too seriously? I know I warned you yesterday to look after yourself, but the sort of accident you've just described is not so rare, you know. People in crowds jostle each other and get impatient and—"

"I'm telling you, I was pushed, Chief Superintendent. But you're right, in a way. I might have thought it was an accident, except for this." He reached into his breast pocket and brought out a small piece of paper. "When I got home, I found this in my overcoat pocket."

Henry took the paper and studied it. It was a page torn from a small, cheap notebook, and the penciled message was printed in shaky block capitals by an apparently uneducated hand. It read: SIMON WARWICK WONT EVER INHERIT SIMON WARWICK WILL DIE.

Henry looked at Harold Benson. He said, "Are you sure you didn't write this yourself, Mr. Benson?"

"Of course I'm sure."

With a small sigh, Henry said, "Very well. We'll assume you didn't. In that case, I don't think what happened this morning was a serious murder attempt. It sounds to me more like a warning."

"I know it," said Benson. "I know it. And that's why I'm bowing out and going home. I'm withdrawing my claim. There's no inheritance that's worth a human life."

Henry said, "So you admit you are not Simon Warwick?"

"I'm admitting nothing. I'm just telling you that Simon Warwick does not exist—at least as far as that will is concerned."

"Are you trying to say that you are Simon Warwick, but you are waiving the right to your inheritance, just because of a cheap threat?"

Benson said again, "Simon Warwick does not exist."

"Does Simon Finch exist, Mr. Benson?"

"He—no. Simon Finch does not exist."

"You mean, he's dead."

"I mean what I say."

"But you knew him once, didn't you? You got that passport from him."

Benson's agitation was distressing. He said, "I refuse to discuss the matter."

"I'm afraid you can't do that, Mr. Benson. You seem to have forgotten that you are an important witness in a murder investigation. Where did you get that passport?"

Benson stood up. "I refuse to answer any more questions without my attorney being present."

"Very well." Henry pressed the buzzer on his desk, and Sergeant Hawthorn appeared at the door, round-faced and smiling. "Sergeant, please take Mr. Benson to a telephone so that he can call his lawyer. Then stay with him in the waiting room until the solicitor arrives. After that, we can go on."

When Benson and Hawthorn had gone, Inspector Reynolds, who had been standing quietly at the back of the room throughout the interview, said, "He's lying, sir."

"Lying about what?" said Henry. "About the attempt on his life? About being Simon Warwick? About *not* being Simon Warwick?"

Reynolds scratched his head. "Blowed if I know, sir. On the face of it, I'd say he wrote that note himself, and made up the whole story, just to try to prove that he *is* Warwick."

"And then denies that he is? Pretty convoluted reasoning."

"I admit it's hard to make head or tail of it, sir, but I just know he's lying."

Henry said, slowly, "I wouldn't have expected him to give up so easily. With Goodman exposed as a fraud, and his documents forged, Benson has produced the only solid piece of evidence there is—the passport. Quince and Hamstone will have to give his claim serious consideration, whatever they may say, before any court will agree to presume that Warwick is dead. Suppose somebody did try to push Benson under a bus, and slipped that note into his pocket? Would you have believed that that young man would have been so intimidated that he's not only prepared to give up his claim, but to lay himself open to very serious charges of misrepresentation as well?"

"You never can tell what will scare people, sir."

"A murder charge," said Henry, "scares most people."

"You're going to arrest him, sir?"

"Well," Henry said, "just consider. He had the motive and the opportunity. He was in that room with Goodman for quite long enough to kill him, and Miss Benedict remembers that Goodman had a copy of the *Times* with him, so that the presence of the newspaper doesn't mean that a third person must have been involved—although that's what Benson will obviously claim." Henry paused. "I may be wrong, Reynolds, but the way I see it now is this. Harold Benson was born Simon Warwick, became Simon Finch and is now calling himself Harold Benson. He dare not admit his identity as Finch for some reason. What reason? Maybe he killed the real Harold Benson and took his identity. When he realized that there was a fortune waiting for Simon Finch-Warwick, he couldn't resist at least having a try at claiming it. He must have been badly rattled by Goodman. He knew he was a fraud, but didn't know how to prove it, since Goodman was impersonating *him*—that is, Simon Finch. If he had, in fact, killed Harold Benson, his impulse to solve matters by murdering Goodman would be more understandable. How does that strike you, Reynolds?"

"Strikes me as pretty likely, sir. Very good reasoning."

"No, it isn't," said Henry, irritably. "It's nearly right, but not quite. Meanwhile, we can't run the risk of Benson—or whatever his name really is—slipping out of the country."

The evening papers announced that a man was at police headquarters helping the CID with their inquiries into the murder of the supposed Simon Finch, now known to have been Ronald Goodman. The following day they carried the story that Harold Benson, Jr., a citizen of the United States, had been arrested and charged with the murder.

Ambrose Quince telephoned Henry Tibbett at his home that evening to congratulate him on solving the case and bringing the murderer to justice.

"Not so fast, Mr. Quince," Henry said. "The man's innocent until he's proved guilty, you know."

"Of course, of course. But the thing's a foregone conclusion, I should imagine. Fellow must be slightly crazy, of course. How he imagined that killing Goodman could possibly help *his* claim to stand up—"

Henry said, "Harold Benson now wishes to withdraw his claim to the estate."

"He . . . what?"

"Apparently somebody tried to push him under a bus and slipped a threatening note into his pocket. He's decided that to be Simon Warwick is altogether too dangerous."

"That's rubbish," said Ambrose promptly.

"Well, Goodman got himself murdered—"

"Ah, yes, but he wasn't married."

"What on earth has that got to do with it?" Henry asked.

"Oh, I forgot. You haven't actually read the new will, have you? Well, if Simon Warwick turns out to be dead, or dies before his claim has been substantiated, the estate goes to his eldest legitimate child. Benson is married and has a son. So killing him wouldn't change matters—if he does turn out to be Simon Warwick after all."

"He now admits that he isn't," said Henry. "He says Simon Warwick doesn't exist."

"We'll see about that," said Ambrose. "Benson has made a formal claim, and it's going to be investigated whether he likes it or not."

"This is rather an abrupt change of attitude, isn't it?" Henry said. "I thought you were all set to get Simon Warwick declared dead."

"So I was," said Ambrose. "But Benson's arrest has changed all that. Between ourselves, Tibbett, Cecily and Crumble and Westbury would be delighted if Harold Benson could be proved to be Simon Warwick."

"They would?"

"Of course. Didn't I tell you that there was a clause in the will disinheriting Warwick if *for any reason* he did not take his seat on the board of directors and take an active part in running the company within three years of Lord Charlton's death? Well, a man serving a life sentence isn't going to take a seat on any board. So the matter would be most conveniently disposed of. Diana Crumble said so in as many words to Rosalie this afternoon when they met at the hairdresser's. It's not going to be a simple matter to get a court of law to presume Warwick's death, and meantime in the next three years more claimants may turn up and the estate will in any case be frozen. No, the sooner the old will comes back into force, the better. I hear Denton's already paid his tailor's bill, and Cecily is talking about having her apartment redecorated. So I thought congratulations were in order. Remember me to Mrs. Tibbett, won't you? And Rosalie sends her regards. Goodnight, Tibbett."

The note found in Harold Benson's pocket was turned over to the police laboratory and a handwriting expert, but proved predictably fruitless. The paper came from the cheapest sort of jotting pad and provided no clues. There were no fingerprints except Benson's own. With Ambrose Quince's cooperation, Henry again visited Lord Charlton's library, where he found and took away specimens of the handwriting of Cecily Smeed, Sir Percy Crumble, and Bertram Hamstone. Inspector Reynolds visited Denton Westbury in the guise of a conservation enthusiast collecting signatures for a petition to preserve Battersea Power Station for posterity, and was embarrassed to be offered a subscription as well as a signature. The handwriting expert concluded sadly that the printing on the note could not be positively identified with any of these specimens, although he gave Henry, unofficially, his own idea of which one it might be. Neither did the writing of the note resemble Harold Benson's own writing.

Benson himself, on the advice of his lawyer—a somewhat pompous young man called Reginald Colby, recommended by Ambrose Quince—refused to add or subtract anything to or from his original statement concerning the death of Ronald Goodman. He refused to discuss the matter of his own identity or that of Simon Finch, beyond the bland statement that the latter did not exist. The police prosecutors prepared their case. And Henry Tibbett worried.

The reason for Henry's worrying was very simple. For one of the very few times in his career, he had arrested a man on a charge of murder without being one hundred percent certain in his own mind that the defendant was guilty. The prosecutors were more than satisfied with the evidence. Susan Benedict was to be their star witness, and she was sticking to her story with admirable fidelity. Inquiries in the United States had unearthed the fact that Harold Benson had taken a course in karate while at college, which gave him one more qualification for conviction. As to the question "Who is Simon Warwick?" the legal experts showed little interest. It really was not germane to the case. Ronald Goodman had been

115

killed because his rival claimant had *believed* him to be Simon Warwick. The fact that Benson now wished to withdraw his claim was seen as a last-minute attempt to remove his motive for murder when he realized that his arrest was imminent. So long as there was sufficient evidence to convince a jury that Harold Benson had killed Ronald Goodman, the question of Simon Warwick's actual identity was neither here nor there.

Knowing all this to be true, Henry Tibbett continued to ponder the question. He arranged unofficial meetings with several of the key figures in the case. With Ambrose Quince; with Lady Diana Crumble, whom he had never met, owing to her prolonged stay in Scotland; with Cecily Smeed. It was on the morning of his appointment with Ambrose Quince that Inspector Reynolds came into Henry's office, looking harassed.

"It's about Benson, sir."

"What about Benson?"

"He's in a fair old state, sir. Really upset. It's about his wife."

"His wife?"

"Mrs. Sally Benson, sir."

"What about her? Has she decided to leave him or something?"

"No, sir. Quite the reverse. She's apparently decided to fly over here to be with him during the trial."

Henry raised his eyebrows. "Very natural and commendable, I should have thought."

"Well, Benson doesn't seem to agree with you, sir. He's demanding to see you, and . . . well, I think it might be a good idea if you had a talk with him."

"Okay, Reynolds. If you say so."

Harold Benson was being held in custody at a remand center in southern England—an establishment that was in no way punitive, seeming to figure somewhere between a public school and a convalescent home, except that the doors were locked to prevent the inmates from leaving. Harold Benson greeted Henry with reassurances that he had no complaints whatsoever about his treatment or his legal representation, and then launched into the topic of his wife's projected visit.

"You've got to stop her, Chief Superintendent. You must. You can do it. She's not to come to England."

Henry said, "Mr. Benson, your wife is of age and a free person. So long as she has a valid passport, I can't possibly stop her from coming here."

"Don't you understand the danger?"

"Danger?"

"Somebody tried to kill me," said Benson. "They can't get at me now, but they can get at her."

Henry smiled, "I know you've got plenty on your mind, Mr. Benson," he said, "but you must keep a sense of proportion. It seems to me that your wife is doing absolutely the right thing in coming over here to be with you. When you see her—"

"I won't see her."

"What do you mean?"

"I've told you," said Harold Benson. "I won't have her coming to this place. If she turns up, she'll be told that I refuse to talk to her."

Henry shrugged. "That's entirely your affair. But I certainly can't stop her from coming."

Angrily, Benson said, "Then you can at least give her police protection."

"Against what, for heaven's sake?"

"Against whoever is trying to kill us."

Henry stood up. "I'm sorry," he said. "I can't prevent your wife from visiting you, nor can I give her police protection against a figment of your imagination. If I were you, I should be thankful that she's coming, and enjoy her visit. When is she expected?"

Benson pushed a piece of paper across the table to Henry. It was a section torn from an aerogram letter, written in a confident, sloping hand. It read: ". . . shall arrive at London Airport at 11:15 a.m. on Tuesday 18th, via Pan Am from Washington. I'm sure you can arrange for me to be met (what are attorneys for??). So that they can identify me, I shall wear my navy-blue suit (so discreet), with a big yellow artificial flower in the lapel, and that yellow and navy silk Hermes scarf that you brought me from Paris last year. Oh, Harry, I can't tell you how much I . . ."

Benson said, "There'll be nobody there to meet her, unless you do it."

Henry replied, "I'm sorry, Mr. Benson, this is quite outside my—"

And Benson said, "Go to hell." Which concluded the interview, leaving Henry holding the scrap of blue airmail paper in his hand.

Henry's detour to the remand center caused him to arrive ten minutes late at Ambrose Quince's office, thus unwittingly throwing the system out of gear. However, Ambrose—who had another appointment later on—contrived to emerge one-up in his own estimation by finding time to make Henry wait a further three minutes, which he judged to be the minimum for satisfying honor without giving the impression of inefficiency. It would have upset him had he realized how few of the people he received were aware of these niceties of timing.

He greeted Henry warmly, asked to what he owed the honor of this visit, and added, "How is our friend Benson these days?"

Henry said, "Fit and well, when I saw him half an hour ago. He's bothered about his wife's visit, but otherwise he seems fine."

"His wife?"

"She's flying over next Tuesday to stand by him during the trial. Very decent of her, I'd have thought, but for some reason he doesn't want to see her. However, that's not what I came to talk about. I'm still interested in Simon Warwick."

"I know you are, old man," said Quince, "but I really don't see how I can help you."

"Your father was the last person I've been able to trace who saw him after he went to America."

"But my father's been dead for years, Tibbett."

"I know that. But did he never mention—?"

Ambrose shook his head. "Old Charlton thought I might have heard something from my father," he said, "but Dad was the proverbial soul of discretion."

Henry said, "That trip that your father took to the United States in 1949—would you have any record of it here in the office?"

"What trip?"

"Didn't you know? Your father saw young Simon Warwick at the age of five, and wrote Lord Charlton a letter about him."

"Oh, that." Ambrose waved a hand. "Yes, I saw that letter. But what more is there to find out? All that part of the research has been done. My father visited the Finches in McLean, Virginia, and saw the boy. That's all there is to it."

"Yes," said Henry. "Yes, I suppose it is."

"Frankly," said Ambrose, "I'm more interested in the fact that Sally Benson is coming to England. I shall be fascinated to meet that young woman."

"You will? Why?"

"Didn't I tell you? She led Rosalie and me right up the garden path when we were in the States."

"What do you mean?"

"Well." Ambrose leaned back and lit a cigarette. "We had an appointment to meet her at the Bensons' house at the university in Charlottesville. We drove all the way down there from

Washington—a couple of hours in filthy weather—to be greeted by a maid and an empty house, and a note telling us that she'd been called away because her son had been taken ill at ski camp, and wouldn't we call and make another date? It was only by the purest chance that we discovered that her son wasn't ill at all, and she hadn't been called away. The woman was simply avoiding us."

"How very strange," said Henry. "Have you any idea why?"

"I've every idea. We were investigating her husband's claim, and she knew bloody well it was fraudulent. She was afraid she might make a slip and give the game away."

Henry said, "And you never made another appointment?"

"We didn't bother. By the next day, we had the Finch situation sewn up and in the bag." Ambrose paused. "Of course, we didn't know then that we had a bogus Finch on our hands."

Still worried, Henry made his way back to his Chelsea flat. Emmy, making preliminary preparations for supper, was bustling about in the kitchen. She listened to Henry's account of his day with polite but preoccupied interest, and only when the subject of Sally Benson was broached did she show a lively reaction.

She said, "Well, what are you going to do, Henry?"

"Do? Nothing, of course."

"But that poor girl . . . coming all this way to a strange country with her husband in prison for murder—"

Henry said, "Do try to be accurate. He's on remand on a charge of murder. That's quite different."

"No, it isn't. At least, I know how I'd feel if it were you," said Emmy, with spirit. "And then you say that he's refusing to see her. What's she going to do, for heaven's sake?"

Henry closed his eyes. "I have no idea," he said. "That's her problem."

"When did you say she was coming?"

"Oh, I forget. Here's the bit of her letter he gave me, if you're so interested. But I'm warning you, Emmy—it would be extremely improper for me to get involved in any way with her visit. Just remember that. Okay?"

Instead of answering, Emmy switched on the liquidizer to make soup. She glanced at the scrap of blue paper. Good strong hand-writing. What are attorneys for? I do so agree, but Benson's not going to do anything about it and nor is his lawyer. The Pan Am flight from Washington at 11:15 next Tuesday morning. Navy-blue suit with a big yellow flower. Don't worry, Sally Benson. Someone will be there to meet you.

12

Henry's second visit to the Crumbles' Down Street house was considerably more successful than the first. It was a quarter past four in the afternoon, and the butler informed Henry that her ladyship was taking tea in the drawing room, and would be pleased if Chief Superintendent Tibbett would join her. As the butler helped him off with his raincoat, Henry took a quick look around the hall and decided that it must have been Lady Diana who had planned the decor of this house. Where Sir Percy's office reflected precisely his taste for brash opulence, here everything was muted and aristocratically understated. A very pretty house. A very feminine house.

The butler opened the drawing-room door (antique brass handle and panels picked out in gold leaf), announced Henry, and stood back to usher him in. The room was as elegant and fragile as the rest of the house, except for the deep, comfortable, and tough-looking Knoll sofa facing the fire. In front of the sofa, on a low table, tea had been laid out on a lace-fringed tablecloth—silver teapot and milk jug, wafer-thin watercress sandwiches, *petits fours*, eggshell china cups, and minuscule lace napkins—and on the sofa, heads together in conversation, sat Lady Diana Crumble and Rosalie Quince.

"Chief Inspector Tibbett! Oh, dear, I've got it wrong, haven't I?"

"Chief Superintendent," said Rosalie.

"Well, whatever it is, come in and sit down. So very nice to meet you—Rosalie has told me such a lot . . . Rotten weather, isn't it . . . hope you didn't get too wet . . . Milk or lemon?"

Lady Diana was very tall and very thin, with a face like a greyhound's: not beautiful, but undoubtedly impressive. Henry, perched uncomfortably on a spindle-legged gilt chair, made suitable noises, greeted Rosalie Quince, accepted tea with milk and a watercress sandwich, and wondered how to begin. He need not have worried. Diana Crumble made it easy for him.

"So you have caught your murderer, Mr. Tibbett. I do congratulate you. Percy says you have done splendidly."

"Thank you," said Henry. "I'm not—"

"So," Diana went on, "it can't be about *that* that you've come to see. I've been having a little bet with Rosalie. She thinks you've come to ask me to give evidence, or some such gruesome thing. But I say you're still worrying about Simon Warwick. Am I right?"

Henry grinned. "You've won your bet, Lady Diana. I'm not here on an official visit at all. I just want to try to get to the bottom of this Simon Warwick business—to satisfy my own curiosity."

Seriously, Diana Crumble said, "We'd all be grateful if you could clear it up, Mr. Tibbett. If it should turn out that Harold Benson really is Simon Warwick—"

"Diana would be delighted," Rosalie put in. "And Percy and Denton and all the rest. But surely it's most unlikely. Ambrose and I visited his home in Leesburg, and —"

"Now, Rosalie, let the chief superintendent get a word in edgewise," said Diana, with gentle reproof. "More tea, Mr. Tibbett? Do try one of these little pink things—they're really delicious. I'm so lucky to have found a Viennese cook. Now—tell us all about Simon Warwick."

Henry said, "I was hoping you might be able to tell me, Lady Diana."

"Tell you—what? I only saw Simon twice—once when he was only a few days old, and then a week or so later when I took him down to Marstone, poor little chap, after his parents were killed. Percy told you about that, didn't he?"

"Yes, he did."

"Mary Cheverton was an old friend of mine, you see. We were at school together. I didn't know Dominic so well, of course, but I saw quite a lot of them after they got married." Henry remembered the wedding photograph, and a younger version of the greyhound face in the background, topped by a uniform cap of some sort. "But of course," Diana went on, "that's not the sort of thing you're interested in."

"I'm interested in anything that could possibly be relevant," Henry said. "I don't suppose you met the adoptive parents when you went to Marstone?"

"No, no. They weren't expected until later in the day. I just left Simon with Mr. Humberton in his office."

"You see," Henry said, "I know so little about Simon Warwick. I know that he was adopted by a couple called Finch who brought him up in McLean, Virginia. I know that he ran away from home when he was fifteen—maybe to England, because later on his adoptive mother came over here and consulted Alfred Humberton. She may well have been looking for Simon. I know that as a small boy he was remarkably like his father but had his mother's eyes. And that's—"

Diana Crumble said, "But he didn't."

Henry stopped in midsentence. "He didn't?"

"No. His eyes were blue."

"I know they were. I've seen the passport he left England on as a baby. Didn't Mary Warwick have blue eyes, then?"

Diana leaned forward and pushed a recalcitrant log into place with a poker. She said, "It was funny. Often people didn't spot it at once. They were just aware that there was something . . . something odd about Mary, but they couldn't put their finger on it until it was pointed out. Then, of course, it became glaringly obvious."

"What did?"

"Mary's eyes. The left one was blue, but the right one was a pale hazely green. She was always very self-conscious about it, and I remember so well, when I went to see her and the baby—I must have been her first visitor, apart from Dominic—I remember her saying how glad she was that little Simon had two good blue eyes. The double coloring is often inherited, you see."

There was a silence. Then Henry said, "Robert Quince—your father-in-law, Mrs. Quince—he knew both Mary and Dominic Warwick, didn't he?"

"Of course," said Diana.

"So when he wrote to Alexander Warwick when Simon was five, after seeing the child in the United States, and specifically mentioned that he had his mother's eyes—he could only have meant that one was blue and the other green."

"But I saw the baby—"

Rosalie said, "All babies are born with blue eyes, aren't they?"

"That's an old wives' tale," Henry said, "but in this case it's perfectly possible that the difference in pigmentation didn't develop until later on. That passport was issued when the child was only two weeks old, after all."

Diana said, "Then Harold Benson isn't Simon Warwick. Nobody we've set eyes on is Simon Warwick, because nobody has two eyes of different colors." She looked at Rosalie. "Ambrose had better put in another advertisement, Rosalie darling. Will all young gentlemen born Simon Warwick, adopted by Captain and Mrs. Finch, and having one blue and one green eye, kindly apply to—"

Rosalie said, "So that's what the old man meant when he said he would recognize his nephew. He might have told Ambrose."

"He certainly might," Henry agreed. "If he had, Ronald Goodman would probably be alive today."

"Wait a moment," said Rosalie suddenly. "I think he did try to tell Ambrose."

"He did?"

"Yes. When he was dying. I suppose he wanted to keep it to himself so long as he thought he would be identifying Simon personally. It's the sort of dramatic effect that he would have enjoyed. He must have thought that he would have at least a few hours before he died to let Ambrose in on the secret. But the heart attack was so sudden, and happened so late at night, that he had no time. The butler told us what he said . . . just three words . . . 'Ambrose, Simon, I . . .'"

"Of course," Henry said, "the butler naturally thought Lord Charlton was saying 'I,' referring to himself. Actually, he must have been trying to leave Ambrose the message about Simon's eyes." He sighed. "Well, there's nothing to be done about it now. It scotches a theory I was playing around with, and it makes it a virtual certainty that Simon Warwick *is* dead. Harold Benson undoubtedly knows a lot more about the real Simon Warwick than he's letting on—including the color of his eyes. I daresay his wife does, too, and that's why he doesn't want her over here."

"He doesn't?" Diana Crumble sounded surprised. "Why not?"

"He fed me a cock-and-bull story about being frightened for her safety. That's nonsense, of course. The fact of the matter is that she knows too much, and he's afraid she'll give something away."

"Which is also why she avoided us in Charlottesville," said Rosalie.

"Obviously." Henry stood up. "Thank you for a delicious tea, Lady Diana. And for a fascinating but highly inconvenient piece of information."

Later that evening, in the Chelsea flat, Henry and Emmy Tibbett sat over steaming mugs of milky coffee, and talked about Simon Warwick.

"I was so sure," Henry said, "So sure that he was alive."

"And now you think he's not?"

"What I think is," Henry said, "that I've got a murderer in custody all right, but for the wrong murder."

"You mean Harold Benson?"

"Of course. I don't believe he killed Goodman, for all the circumstantial evidence. I do believe he killed Simon Finch—a number of years ago." He rubbed the back of his neck with his hand. "It's a nice problem in ethics, isn't it? Do I let him be justly punished, but for the wrong crime? Or do I blow up my own case against him and let him go free?"

"Isn't there any other way?" Emmy said.

"Only one. Only one really moral way. Get him acquitted on the Goodman charge, and dig up enough evidence, going back twenty years or so and in another country, to convict him of killing Finch."

Emmy said, "What makes you so sure he didn't kill Goodman?"

"Only a hunch. If he knew the real Simon Finch, then he must have known Goodman was a phony. Still . . . I suppose he might have killed him. I just don't know, Emmy. Let's go to bed."

The following evening, Henry went by appointment to pay a call on Cecily Smeed. Over the telephone, she had been cool, businesslike, and apparently unsurprised that Henry wished to talk to her. As soon as he arrived at the Kensington apartment, however, she opened the proceedings by saying, "I really can't imagine what you can have to say to me, Chief Superintendent. After all, you have arrested Harold Benson, whom I have never even met. I can't think why you waited so long. It was perfectly obvious from the beginning that he was guilty."

"Was it, Miss Smeed? Where did you get that idea from?"

"Oh, Ambrose and Percy Crumble and the Hamstones. They've all been talking about it, naturally."

Henry said, "They could only have got their information from Mr. Quince, and he isn't in possession of all the facts. However, it seems that for once uninformed rumor may turn out to be right."

"Well, in that case—"

"Miss Smeed," Henry said, "I didn't come here to talk about Harold Benson or the murder. I came to ask you to tell me your precise connection with Denton Westbury. For a start, I think you can tell me his real name."

Cecily was completely taken aback. She went very pale, and did not answer for a moment. Then she said, "I don't know what you mean. I have come across the young man quite often in the course of business, that's all."

"I don't think it is all, Miss Smeed. When he came to London seven years ago, apparently knowing nobody, you took him up in a big way. You introduced him to Lord Charlton and other important people, and I strongly suspect that you set him up in business as an interior decorator. Why?"

Cecily said, "That has nothing to do with the case."

"That's for me to decide," Henry said. And then, "Is he your son?"

"Certainly not!" The words came out with spontaneous vehemence. Then, very quietly, Cecily said, "He is my nephew. His real name is Alexander Smeed."

"Your brother's son?"

A long pause. Then Cecily said, "No, Mr. Tibbett. Denton is the son of my late sister. She was unmarried. You realize that I am telling you this in strict confidence, and I beg you not to let it go any further."

Henry said, "I'll repay your confidence with one of my own, Miss Smeed. Did you hear that somebody tried to push Benson under a bus and left a threatening note in his pocket? It happened shortly before he was arrested."

Almost inaudibly, Cecily said, "Ambrose mentioned something about it. Benson made the whole thing up, didn't he, and wrote the note himself?"

"I turned the note over to our handwriting expert, Miss Smeed," Henry said, "together with specimens of writing from various other people concerned. He wasn't able to make a positive identification—nothing that would stand up in court. However, he did tell me two things privately. One was that Benson had certainly not written the note himself, and the other was that in his opinion the note was probably written by Denton Westbury."

Cecily shook her head despairingly. "The little fool," she said. "The little fool."

"I don't take the so-called murder attempt very seriously," Henry said. "Nobody meant to kill Benson, because it would have done no good as far as restoring the old will was concerned. Benson is married and has a son, who would have inherited after his father's death, provided Benson was proved to have been Simon Warwick. No, I think somebody was trying to frighten Benson into withdrawing his claim. In that, they have succeeded."

Cecily looked up sharply. "They have?"

"Benson is withdrawing his claim. But that makes very little difference, because I now have definite proof that he is not Simon Warwick." There was a pause. Cecily sat quite still, never taking her eyes off Henry. He went on, "You knew Dominic Warwick, of course, Miss Smeed. Did you ever meet his wife?"

"No, never. What a curious question, Mr. Tibbett. Why do you ask?"

"Never mind. I just wanted to be sure. Now, you say that Mr. Westbury's real name is Alexander Smeed. Have you any idea who his father is—or was?"

"Oh, for heaven's sake, stop beating about the bush, Mr. Tibbett. You must have guessed long ago. It was Lord Charlton, of course."

This time it was Henry who found himself momentarily without a reply. Then he said, "No, Miss Smeed, I hadn't guessed. Did he know?"

"He didn't, and neither does Denton. I am the only person who knows." Cecily was pacing up and down the big drawing room. "Marjorie was my older sister. She was a very pretty girl. We shared a small flat in the days when I first went to work for Mr. Alexander. She used to come and pick me up at the office sometimes. Mr. Alexander took a fancy to her. I did try to warn her. He used to take up with various . . . women. It never lasted. That was just his way. He always treated them very generously—gave them jewelry and so on, and quite a large sum of money when he finally sent them packing."

"You knew a lot about Lord Charlton's private life, Miss Smeed?"

Cecily smiled, a little grimly. "You'd be amazed at some of the duties of a private secretary, Mr. Tibbett. However, that all came later, when Mr. Alexander grew really rich. In Marjorie's case, it was a young man's passing affair. He grew tired of her, as I knew he would. He found her a very good job up in the Midlands—not with

126

his own company, of course—and that was that. He never knew that she was pregnant, and it would have been as much as my job was worth to tell him."

"It's ironic," said Henry, "to think that he was searching for his nephew, when all the time his own natural son was—"

Cecily seemed not to have heard. She went on. "After Marjorie died, I brought the boy to London. I was determined that his father should do something to help him, whether he was aware of it or not."

"It didn't occur to you to tell him then, after the boy was grown up?"

Cecily gave Henry a pitying look. "Of course it occurred to me," she said, "until I found out what Denton had become. Can you imagine Mr. Alexander turning control of Warwick Industries over to a homosexual interior decorator? Don't be silly. If the boy had been different . . . more of Mr. Alexander's idea of a son . . . I might have risked it. As it was, I decided to play it the other way. We invented the name Denton Westbury—I didn't want Denton to have any apparent family connection with me—and I persuaded Mr. Alexander to let him do the Belgrave Terrace house. But I'm afraid he wasn't really very good. Mr. Alexander had it redone the following year. Still, it had given Denton a good introduction to London society, so we got started on charity fund raising, and that went much better. And with the job at the Charlton Foundation, he would have been set up for life. In fact, he *will* be set up for life, unless the real Simon Warwick turns up. Oh, the idiot! Now I suppose you'll arrest him and—"

Henry held up his hand. "Miss Smeed, why do you think I came to see you, instead of going to Westbury? I told you, I have no evidence that would convince a jury. No harm has been done, and I don't intend to take any further action. I just wanted to be sure in my own mind. It's another piece of a very complicated jigsaw puzzle falling into place."

Very quietly, Cecily said, "You are very kind."

Henry stood up. "I must warn you about one thing, though, Miss Smeed."

"Warn me?"

"Benson hasn't yet been proved guilty of the murder of Goodman. If it should turn out that he is innocent after all, and if either you or Westbury had anything to do with it—well, further action will certainly be taken."

At 11:15 the following Tuesday morning, Henry Tibbett was in his office, dealing with preliminary evidence on a new case and thinking about Harold Benson and Simon Warwick. And Emmy Tibbett was at the terminal at Heathrow Airport that welcomes—if that is the word—transatlantic visitors. She had parked her small car in a distant and inconvenient garage, and was now searching among the arrivals for a lady in a navy-blue suit with a yellow flower in her buttonhole.

As a matter of fact, Emmy saw her almost immediately. Sally Benson, tall and graceful, with a drift of blonde hair, light makeup, and huge dark glasses, was conspicuous among the somewhat frazzled passengers making their way through customs and immigration toward the freedom of England's green and pleasant land. The trouble was that too many other people were meeting too many other people. Among the throng of friends and relatives were uniformed chauffeurs of hired cars, holding up sheets of paper on which the names of their passengers were written in bold letters; suddenly, Emmy noticed that one of them read MRS. HAROLD BENSON.

There was a barrier between arriving passengers and welcoming friends, and Emmy fought her way through the crowd toward it, calling out, "Mrs. Benson! Mrs. Benson!" She had nearly reached the barrier when Sally Benson came through it, stopped and looked around her, obviously trying to locate someone. It occurred to Emmy that it was very silly to wear dark glasses on a February morning in London, and at the same moment the identical idea seemed to occur to Sally Benson. She put her hand to her forehead and momentarily took off her dark glasses; and in that short moment, Emmy saw quite clearly that one of her eyes was blue, and the other a pale hazel green.

Then as a wall of struggling humanity pushed itself between Emmy and Mrs. Benson, Emmy glimpsed the back of the uniformed chauffeur. Weaving deftly among the crowd, he reached Mrs. Benson, saluted, and said something that Emmy could not catch. Sally smiled brilliantly and replaced her dark glasses, and the next moment the chauffeur had relieved her of her hand baggage and was escorting her to the far exit. As she tried frantically to follow, Emmy cannoned into a massive lady in tweeds, who said icily, "There's no need to push, you know."

"Excuse me. I'm sorry. I'm in a great hurry."

"I'm sure we're *all* in a hurry," remarked the large lady, as she sailed past Emmy in the opposite direction. Emmy reached the exit just in time to see the chauffeur climb into the driving seat of a big black limousine. Sally Benson's blonde head was visible through the rear window. All that Emmy could do was to make a note of the car's registration number before it pulled smoothly away from the curb and disappeared down the exit road from the airport.

"Mrs. Tibbett is on the line, Chief Superintendent," announced the telephone operator at Scotland Yard. "She would like to speak to you."

Henry, his thread of thought broken by the ringing telephone, said irritably, "Tell her I'm busy. I'll see her at lunchtime."

"Very good, Chief Superintendent."

Henry went back to his papers, annoyed. Emmy knew very well that he did not like her calling him in his office, and in any case he would be seeing her in just over an hour.

The telephone rang again. "Excuse me, Chief Superintendent, but Mrs. Tibbett says it's very urgent. She must speak to you."

"Oh, very well. Put her through. Emmy? What's all this about? . . . You're *where*? . . . What are you doing there, for God's sake? . . . Well, you had no business to. I told you the other day that it would be most improper . . . What? . . . Say that again . . . Have you taken leave of your senses, woman? How could she possibly be? . . . You mean, you think she's his daughter, or something . . .?"

"Henry," said Emmy, uncomfortably aware of the lack of privacy in the airport telephone kiosk, "I'm trying to tell you. Harold Benson didn't kill Simon Warwick. He *married* him."

"Are you crazy?"

"No, I—my God, Henry, she's come back into the terminal . . . must have forgotten a piece of luggage, or something . . . Have you got the car number? PJ8745X. Big black hire car, by the look of it. There she goes. I'm going after her . . ."

The line went dead.

13

For a moment, Henry sat looking at the telephone in his hand. Then he hung up, and called Inspector Reynolds on the intercom.

"I want a car traced, Reynolds. Large black limousine, number PJ8745X. Get someone onto identifying the owner, and put out a call to all squad cars in the vicinity of Heathrow Airport. If anybody spots the car—it just left the airport—report back here, and tail it. No, I don't want it stopped, not at this stage. Driver is a uniformed chauffeur, passenger a blonde woman. Possibly there may be a dark woman in the car as well. Got that? Good. Then come in here, will you? I want to talk to you."

Five minutes later, Inspector Reynolds was facing Henry across the desk, his square, honest face displaying bafflement and incredulity.

"I can't believe it, sir."

"I couldn't for about a minute," Henry said, grinning. "Then, as I thought about it, everything fell into place. Sex-change operations aren't all that usual, of course, but they've been going on quietly for a long time, and there are more of them every year. I remember reading somewhere that a hospital in Baltimore, is especially famous for them. Harold Benson went to college in Washington, D.C., which isn't far from Baltimore."

"But, sir—" Reynolds was still struggling with disbelief. "The Bensons have a son."

"So did the Finches," Henry pointed out.

"Oh—yes, I see what you mean. The boy may be adopted."

"Must be, if we're right," Henry said. "Doctors can turn a man into a woman physiologically, but not even the greatest surgeons have been able to transplant reproductive organs—so far."

"So when Benson said that Simon Finch didn't exist—"

"He was telling the exact truth," said Henry. "After the operation, the woman—as she now is—is issued with a complete new set of documents, including birth certificate, in her new name and with her new sex. I wonder what the lawyers will make of it. Simon Warwick is alive—yet Simon Warwick no longer exists. Nor does Simon Finch. He became Sally Finch sometime in the 1960s." He paused. "Simon Finch never ran away from home, of course. He went to start a new life as a girl—to his father's shame and fury, but, I imagine, with his mother's sympathy. And then—"

He was interrupted by the telephone. Reynolds answered it. "You have? Good." He began making jottings on a notepad. "Yes . . . that's what we thought . . . Yes, I've got that . . . He did? Where? I see . . . What's that? . . . Nobody? . . . Hold on a moment . . ." He put his hand over the telephone and said to Henry, "Hawthorn's traced the car, sir. Belongs to a big hire firm in Hammersmith—Limitless Limousines. And a squad car has just called in that it's following it now, proceeding along Great West Road in the direction of London . . . not the M4, the old road . . . but there are no passengers, only the driver."

"No passengers?"

"That's what he says, sir."

"Then tell him to flag it down and get information from the driver. Name of hirer, destination, what happened to the passenger . . . he can say it's in connection with a missing person . . ."

Inspector Reynolds gave his instructions, rang off, and then said, "Mrs. Tibbett . . . that is, you said she was going to follow the Benson woman . . . I wonder where she is, sir?" Reynolds and Emmy were old friends.

"So do I," said Henry

"Maybe she'll call again and tell us," said Reynolds hopefully.

But when the telephone rang again, it was Detective Sergeant Hawthorn with the squad-car report. The car had been hired in the name of Reginald Colby, with instructions to meet a Mrs. Benson arriving at Heathrow Airport from Washington at 11:15 A.M. The driver, one Herbert Carter, had located his passenger by the usual

131

method of holding up a card with her name on it. She was a blonde lady wearing a dark blue suit. His instructions were to drop the lady at Mr. Colby's office in Hounslow—only a few miles from the airport. Sixty-one, High Street, Hounslow, to be exact.

The driver had met Mrs. Benson all right, and taken her out to the car, but before they'd gone more than a few yards she found she was missing a piece of hand baggage—one of those airline canvas bags—and she made him go back. Well, of course, it's all one-way at the airport, so it took a little time, but he got her back to the terminal and she wasn't gone more than a couple of minutes. Came back carrying the bag, and just as she was getting into the car, another lady came running out of the building—yes, a dark-haired lady, round about forty, he'd guess. He didn't catch what the dark lady said, but he heard Mrs. Benson say something like, "Oh, that is kind, but my husband's lawyer has sent a car for me"—and then, "Why, of course, I'd be delighted. Do get in." So both ladies got into the car and he drove them to Hounslow. No, they hadn't talked much. The dark lady said Mrs. Benson must be terribly worried, and Mrs. Benson said yes, she was, but she had always heard that British justice was wonderfully fair, and she knew her husband was innocent. In fact, she said, she had come over to prove it. The dark lady asked Mrs. Benson who was her husband's lawyer, and Mrs. Benson said it was a Mr. Reginald Colby.

By that time, they'd arrived in High Street, and as they pulled up outside Number 61, there was a small green Morris parked at the curb. No, he had no idea of the number, never thought to look. And a girl got out of it—hard to describe, really—fairish hair, round about between twenty and thirty probably, Mr. Carter hadn't really noticed. She'd seemed a bit surprised to see two ladies instead of one. The ladies had got out of the car, and Herbert Carter was driving it back to the garage in Hammersmith, when the squad car flagged him down. No, he didn't know whether the three ladies had gone into the building or got into the green Morris. They were standing talking on the pavement when he drove off.

Henry said, "Find out what goes on at 61, High Street, Hounslow."

"Very good, sir."

Five minutes later, Hawthorn reported back. Number 61 was a grocer's shop.

"With offices above it?"

"No, sir. Dwellinghouse, occupied by the grocer, a Mr. Hunt.

132

It's one of the few family businesses left in the neighborhood. Mrs. Hunt has been in all morning, and had no visitors."

Henry relayed this information to Derek Reynolds, and for a moment they looked at each other in silence. Then Henry said, "Goddammit."

"Yes, sir," said Reynolds.

"My bloody fool of a wife," said Henry.

Reynolds cleared his throat. "I think she's done very well, sir, and she's certainly got guts."

Henry said, "She and Simon-Sally Benson and a blonde who may or may not have some connection with Reginald Colby have disappeared into thin air in an anonymous green Morris. She must be out of her mind."

Reynolds said, "Whoever hired that limousine—and it probably wasn't Mr. Colby, but someone giving his name—whoever did that must have intended to kidnap Mrs. Benson, sir. It seems Benson was right to be worried."

Angrily, Henry said, "Of course he was right. He knew his wife was Simon Warwick, and he knew his son was adopted and so couldn't inherit. He knew somebody was out to kill Simon Warwick."

"Well." Reynolds cleared his throat again. "That may be more difficult with Mrs. Tibbett along, mayn't it sir?"

"Somebody," Henry said, "killed Ronald Goodman. Somebody tried to kill Harold Benson—or at least to give him a severe fright."

"The same person, sir?"

"I don't know. I don't think so, but I can't be sure. The fact remains that somebody is also prepared to dispose of Sally Benson. What difference would one more make?"

"Mrs. Tibbett," said Reynolds carefully, "would be missed. She's . . . she's your wife, sir. She's conspicuous."

Abruptly, Henry stood up and smiled at the inspector. "You're a great comfort, Reynolds."

Mr. Reginald Colby, whose offices were, of course, not in Hounslow but in Gray's Inn Road, denied emphatically over the telephone that he had ordered a hired car to meet Mrs. Benson at the airport. He had wished to do so, he told Henry, but his client had been adamant on the subject, and he hardly felt he could fly in the face of definite instructions. In any case, he explained, Benson had told him that it was unlikely that his wife would come to

England after all, in view of a letter that he had written her.

However, when Mrs. Benson showed no signs of canceling her trip, he had taken the liberty of booking a room for her at the London Metropole Hotel, and had cabled her to that effect. Benson had not specifically forbidden him to do so, and it seemed only civil. He was planning to visit her at the hotel later in the day, when he could get away, and he admitted he was not looking forward to meeting her. Why? Well, he would have to tell the poor woman that her husband refused to see her, and wished her to return to the United States on the next available flight.

Henry said, "Did anybody besides you know that Mrs. Benson was booked at the Metropole, but wasn't being met at the airport?"

"Well—my secretary, of course. She made the booking. And . . . yes, now I come to think of it, several other people. I ran into Percy Crumble at Rule's yesterday—he was lunching with Ambrose Quince and Bertie Hamstone and that Westbury fellow. Something to do with the Charlton estate, I suppose. I stopped at their table for a chat, and naturally the subject of Benson came up, and . . . well, yes, I did mention the arrangements I'd made for his wife."

Limitless Limousines came up with the information that the car had been ordered by telephone at 9:48 P.M. the previous evening. No, the office was not open at that hour, but there was a telephone operator on duty at nights who took messages and left them on the booking clerk's desk for the morning. The message had recorded the booking in the name of Mr. Reginald Colby, and a note was added that Mr. Colby's secretary would call at the office before 10 A.M. in the morning, and prepay in cash. The cashier confirmed that this had been done. No, he couldn't possibly identify the person who had paid. Clients paying cash simply pushed the money and their invoice through a grille; he checked that the amount was right, receipted the bill, and pushed it back again, keeping one copy for office use. He never even looked at the person paying. All he knew was that the account had been settled, and the garage told to go ahead and send the car.

Henry hung up and turned to Reynolds. "It has to be one of them. One of the people who stand to gain by the old will being reinstated."

"The person who killed Ronald Goodman," said Reynolds.

"I'm not assuming that yet," Henry said. "What I'm going to do now is to check on every member of that group. At the very least, there should be a break in normal behavior patterns somewhere. Get tails put on all of them, will you? Now, give me that phone . . ."

Sir Percy Crumble was in his office, about to leave for an important business luncheon, Henry was informed by a crisp secretarial voice. When asked if she were Sir Percy's secretary, the voice replied brusquely that she was *one* of Sir Percy's secretaries. Finally convinced by the magic invocation of Scotland Yard, the voice connected Henry with Sir Percy Crumble, who was predictably affable and ignorant.

"What? Me send a car to meet Mrs. Ruddy Benson at Loondon Airport? Are you crazy, Mr. Tibbett? . . . Yes, I remember meeting Reggie Colby at Rule's . . . Did 'e? Well, if 'e did, I don't recall . . . Now, if you'll excuse me, I've an appointment . . ."

It was a bright, brisk February day, and Sir Percy waved aside his chauffeur-driven car and walked through the streets of Mayfair to the expensive restaurant where he was lunching, thus making easy the task of the plainclothes detective who was following him.

When Henry phoned, Lady Diana Crumble was at home, entertaining Miss Cecily Smeed to lunch—a social activity that would have displeased Sir Percy, had he known about it. The fact was that Diana found Cecily, with her infinite knowledge of Warwick Industries, extremely useful from time to time. She also found her quite amusing, and a mine of information on the doings of Barbara Telford, whom Diana had cordially disliked ever since the long-ago year of their debuts into London society. The two women, of course, never discussed the affairs of Amalgamated Textiles. That, Diana knew, would be classed by Cecily as disloyalty to her present employer.

Diana spoke to Henry on the telephone, and laughed uproariously at the idea that she might have ordered a car to meet Sally Benson at the airport.

"I had no idea when she was supposed to be arriving," she said. "All I know is what you told us the other day—that she was planning to come over, and Benson was trying to stop her. Of course I've never met her—what a fantastic idea. What's happening? . . . You've *lost* her? Now I do call that careless—whatever is Scotland Yard coming to? Wait till I tell Cecily . . . Yes, of course you may, if you want to . . ." Her voice grew faint as she spoke away from the telephone. "Cecily, Chief Inspector Tibbett wants a word with you . . . Don't ask me . . . To make sure you're really here, I suppose . . ."

135

"Chief Superintendent Tibbett? This is Cecily Smeed . . . Of course, if I can . . . But I told you the other day I never met Mary Warwick . . . Naturally I'm sure . . . I knew Mr. Dominic, of course, because he used to work in the office . . . Well, when I say *work*, he honored us with a visit from time to time. But after he got married, he didn't consider us grand enough for . . . Yes, Diana, I'm coming. Please excuse me, Mr. Tibbett, I have to go. Luncheon is served."

The pretty house on Down Street had a back door leading into a small cobbled mews, as well as the pale blue front door with the brass knocker in the form of a clenched fist; so it was watched by two detectives.

Mr. Denton Westbury was not at home, and the young Cockney voice that answered the Battersea telephone number sounded at once bored and cheeky. He'd no idea where Denton was. Up west with one of his la-di-dah friends, no doubt. Oh, yes, he'd be *back* all right, but *when*—? "Well, it's no good asking me chum. I don't care if you are Scotland bloody Yard. Wot I don't know I can't tell. Get it?"

"Better have the Battersea house watched," Henry said to Reynolds, "and get someone onto tracing Westbury. I know it won't be easy. Let's try the Hamstones."

Bertram Hamstone was taking a sandwich lunch in his office, due to pressure of work. He had been there all morning and would be there all afternoon. He had nobody with him except his personal secretary, who was taking dictation of a confidential nature. There was, the switchboard at Sprott's Bank informed Henry, absolutely no question of interrupting Mr. Hamstone. Another plainclothes detective took up his station.

The Surrey police reported with commendable speed. A constable had been sent round to The Hollyhocks on the pretext of a security check. The Rolls was outside the garage, being cleaned with loving care by Martin, the chauffeur. The driveway of the house was cluttered with cars, for the good reason that the fundraising committee of the local Church Ladies' Society was being entertained to a buffet lunch by Mrs. Hamstone.

The telephone at Quince, Quince, Quince and Quince was answered by Mr. Silverstein's secretary. Miss Benedict, she said, had taken an early lunch hour, on account of her mother being up from the country for some shopping. She should be back in the office around half-past one. Mr. Quince was in court all day. No, she really couldn't say what case. She worked for Mr. Silverstein, not Mr. Quince. Miss Benedict could tell Inspector Reynolds all about it when she came back.

"That's a nuisance," said Henry, "I wanted to talk to Ambrose Quince. The girl didn't know which court or what the case is?"

"She said she didn't, sir."

Henry thought for a moment, then dialed a number.

"Mrs. Quince? It's Henry Tibbett. I'm sorry to bother you, but I need to speak to your husband, and I understand he's in court."

"That's right. The Westchester divorce case. Rather messy. It's been going on the best part of a week."

"Can you tell me which court it's being heard in?" Henry asked.

"No, I'm afraid I . . . Oh, wait a minute. It'll be in the paper. Just a moment while I look it up. Yes, here's the report of yesterday's proceedings. Let's see. The Law Courts—that's the place in the Strand, isn't it? Court number five Mr. Justice Bilberry."

"Thanks a lot, Mrs. Quince," said Henry. "I think I'll go along and see if I can talk to Ambrose during the luncheon recess."

"Did that woman arrive, by the way?" Rosalie asked. "Benson's wife?"

"I haven't seen her," said Henry, truthfully.

"I just wondered," said Rosalie.

The London Metropole Hotel reported that they had a room reserved in the name of Mrs. Harold Benson, but that she had not yet checked in. As soon as she did, they would ask her to contact Chief Superintendent Tibbett or Inspector Reynolds at Scotland Yard.

Henry was just putting on his raincoat, with the idea of going to the Law Courts and seeking out Ambrose Quince, when Derek Reynolds came into his office, looking worried.

"I've just had the governor of Cragley Remand Center on the line, sir."

"What's happened? Is Benson—?"

"Oh, he's all right, sir. Very pleased, the governor said. You see, there's been a telegram."

"A telegram?"

"For Benson—but naturally it had to go through the governor. Handed in at Charlottesville, Virginia. Message reads"— Reynolds consulted a paper in his hand—" 'Visit canceled love Sally.' Name of sender, Mrs. Benson."

Henry said, "Get Benson here right away."

"If the woman who arrived wasn't Mrs. Benson—" Reynolds began.

"Cables can be faked," Henry said. "A phone call to a friend in the States . . . make some sort of plausible explanation . . . it's not so difficult. Well, this clinches your kidnap theory. But for Emmy, people in the States would have assumed Sally Benson to be in England, while everyone here believed she'd stayed at home in Charlottesville. A huge hotel like the Metropole isn't going to worry about a no-show. It would have been quite some time before anybody realized that the wretched woman was missing. Get Benson to my office at once."

14

For a man with a charge of murder hanging over his head, Harold Benson seemed surprisingly cheerful. When Henry had dismissed the escorting prison officer, and had assured Benson that they were quite alone and that their conversation was not being overheard or recorded, Benson sat down, smiled broadly, and said, "Thank you, Chief Superintendent."

"What for?"

"For heading Sally off. I don't know how you did it, but I sure am grateful. It's a weight off my mind."

Henry said, "I haven't got time for this sort of nonsense, Benson. Why didn't you tell me your wife was Simon Warwick?"

Benson's jaw dropped in utter astonishment. At last, he said, "Now, that's the most absurd—"

"It's not absurd, and you know it. Simon Warwick—or rather, Simon Finch—had a sex-change operation and became Sally Finch. You married her. There's no point in denying it, because I can easily enough check the record of your marriage in the States."

This time, Benson said, "How in heaven's name did you find out?"

"That doesn't matter. What color are your wife's eyes?"

"Oh," said Benson. "Yes, I see. That's the only thing we were afraid of—that somebody might know about the eyes."

"I think," said Henry, "that you'd better tell me about it from the beginning."

"Okay." Benson seemed more at ease. "Since you know, there can't be any harm in it. Of course, I can only tell you what Sally told me. It seems that as far back as she can remember, she somehow knew that nature had made an awful mistake—had put a girl into a boy's body. You may find that hard to believe, but I didn't, when she told me, because Sally is just the most feminine person you can imagine. That's one of the reasons I fell in love with her."

"So Simon Finch had a pretty unhappy childhood," Henry said.

"Miserable. She . . . or he, I suppose, but I just can't think of Sally as anything but a girl . . . he was a bright child, but couldn't get on with the other kids at school. Things weren't made any easier by his father, who was a super-masculine thug with an artificial leg acquired in the war. Naturally, he wanted his son to be super-masculine, too, and do all the things he couldn't. Finally, when he was fifteen, Simon had a complete breakdown. The father dismissed it as hysterical tantrums, but fortunately the mother decided to consult an analyst—a very advanced and perceptive man. He diagnosed the trouble—that is, he got Simon to trust him to the point where he could talk about his problem. The doctor spoke to Mrs. Finch, and advised two things. First, that Simon should be told that Finch was not his real father. That's when Mrs. Finch showed Simon the Warwick passport, and told him who he really was. I don't think she ever knew that Sally took it with her when she left home. It meant so much, you see. Secondly, the doctor advised the sex-change operation. It was rarer then than it is now, of course, but the doctor felt that this was a case in which the poor kid would never be able to lead any sort of a happy life as a boy. He said the sooner the change process was started, the better."

"The change process? I thought it was an operation?"

"That's only the final stage. It's a long job. You can't just walk into the hospital as a man and come out ten days later as a woman. There have to be years of hormone treatment, and gradual changeover, before surgery can be done. Sally was overjoyed at the idea. Mrs. Finch agreed. You can imagine the reaction of Captain Finch. He always called himself Captain, even though it was only a wartime rank. That was the sort of man he was."

Henry nodded. "So what happened?"

"Well," said Benson, "Sally's mother told her the story of the

140

adoption—including the fact that her real mother had had different-colored eyes. Apparently she got that information from some English attorney who had known the Warwicks, and had visited the Finches when Sally was a small child. Mrs. Finch did point out to Sally that she had a very rich bachelor uncle in England who might one day want to trace his nephew, and might be very put out to find a niece instead. Sal said she didn't care. She wanted the operation anyway.

"If Finch had been a different sort of man, it would all have been easy. The whole family could have moved to a new neighborhood, and Sally could have started life there as a girl. But the captain wasn't having any of that. If the boy wished to disgrace the family and drag his father's name in the mud, he said, so much the worse for Simon. He could get out—leave home—never show his face again . . . you can imagine how it was. Finally it was decided that Simon should go and live in Washington—it's only a few miles from McLean, over the river. There, he'd be close to home, and also within easy reach of the Baltimore hospital and the doctor who would eventually do the operation. Mrs. Finch kept in touch all the time, of course. But Captain Finch insisted on putting out the story that his rapscallion son had run away from home—and Mrs. Finch had to go along with it in front of anybody who had known Simon as a boy. The whole emphasis was on making a fresh start, you see."

Henry said, "I had a feeling all along that Simon Finch wasn't a runaway, but I must admit that nothing as bizarre as the real explanation ever occurred to me. Go on."

"Well, Sally lived in an apartment in D.C. and took the hormone treatment and dressed as a girl. She was tremendously happy for the first time in her life. She got excellent grades in school, and after she graduated she had the operation. When she had fully recovered, she entered George Washington University—as a girl, of course, with a fresh set of papers showing that she was, and always had been, Sally Finch. Simon Finch had ceased to exist."

Henry said, "You met at university, did you? You're almost exactly the same age."

"That's right. And both our mothers were English—not that that was any rarity, for people of our generation. My mother used to call it reverse lend-lease—the stream of GI brides coming over from England at the end of the war. Anyhow, it made a sort of bond between us. We started dating, and finally I asked her to marry me.

That was when she told me the truth. Nobody else in the world knew it, except her mother and her doctor. Captain Finch had died the year before."

"Were you upset . . . shocked . . .?" Henry had forgotten that he was a policeman interviewing a murder suspect. He was quite simply fascinated by the story.

Harold Benson smiled, remembering. "I sure as hell was surprised," he said. "As for being upset—well, that was only about myself, not about Sally."

"How do you mean?"

"Well, my first reaction was to suspect I must be a latent homosexual. I'd never felt any interest sexually in other guys—but now it seemed I was asking one to marry me. But Sally made me go and talk to her doctor, and he explained. A homosexual doesn't want to be a woman, see? He enjoys being male, and making love to other men. A transsexual, like Sally, is quite different. He hates his male body. He—or rather she—is a complete, heterosexual woman after the operation. Even before it, a transsexual *feels* like a woman—but a woman trapped in a male body. That's why it always leads to misery if a transsexual experiments with homosexuality. The two are completely different, just as transvestites are something else again."

Henry said, "You're quite an authority on the subject."

Benson grinned. "I had to become one," he said, "before we could get married. I had to be sure I knew what I was doing and felt easy about it. Of course, we can never have children of our own, so we decided from the beginning to adopt at least one. We waited to get married until I was offered this job in Charlottesville. We reckoned it was far enough away from anybody who might possibly have known Sally as Simon. Sally's mother was marvelous to us. It broke Sal's heart that she didn't live to see us married."

"She was killed in an air crash, wasn't she?" said Henry.

"Yes. And Sally has always felt that it was her fault."

"Her fault?"

"Not really, of course, but if it hadn't been for Sally and our engagement, Mrs. Finch would never have been on that airplane. You see, with the wedding coming up, she began to think again about the legal position of Simon Warwick, and she decided to go over to England and consult with the lawyer who arranged the adoption in the first place."

"Humberton?"

"I never knew his name, nor did Sally. However, Mrs. Finch said she was going to tell the attorney the whole story, and get his opinion on the legal situation, should Lord Charlton ever start looking for his nephew. I know she saw him, because she wrote us a very guarded letter from England, saying she would explain the position when she got back home. And then the plane crashed, and we never did find out what the attorney said."

"But Ronald Goodman probably did," said Henry. And then, "What did you think when you heard that your rival claimant was Simon Finch?"

"I didn't," Benson protested. "Quince never told me there was another claimant until that last letter he wrote, and then he didn't give his name. The first time I heard it was from that dumb girl in the outer office. 'Mr. Finch has already arrived,' she said. It gave me almost as big a shock as when I found his body a few moments later. I just couldn't figure it out, until you told me he was the attorney's clerk."

Henry said, "You knew he wasn't Simon Warwick, and he knew that you weren't. Quite an intriguing situation—but somebody made sure it didn't develop."

"Not me, Chief Superintendent. Not me."

"We'll see about that," Henry said. "Meanwhile, how did you come to be making your own fraudulent claim?"

Benson said, "I don't think you can call it fraudulent. Sally saw the advertisement as soon as it appeared, and we talked the whole thing over. We presumed that Lord Charlton knew about his nephew's eyes, so he would have had to acknowledge Sally—but of course then the whole story would have come out, and can you imagine the publicity it would have gotten? Our lives would have been wrecked. But then Lord Charlton died. We talked it all over again. After all, Sally was the rightful heir, absolutely entitled to the money. We felt for our son's sake we ought to try to claim it. I decided to have a shot at it.

"I had to gamble on the fact that nobody but Charlton knew about the eyes—if he'd told the attorney, then I'd have been thrown out at once. It was obvious from the advertisements that Quince didn't know the name of the adoptive parents, so I guessed the other old attorney must be dead and the papers destroyed. I couldn't call myself Finch, of course—I had to sort of graft Sal's story onto my own childhood, which I knew could be checked. The birth date wasn't quite right, but we thought up a story to cover

143

that. It didn't seem to us that it was really a deception. After all, Simon Warwick would have inherited Warwick Industries, which was what Lord Charlton wanted."

"I don't think this is the moment to go into the ethics of the matter," Henry said. "The fact is that you came over to England impersonating your own wife, and Goodman turned up claiming to be Simon Finch. Ambrose Quince went over to the States and did a neat little piece of detective work which proved conclusively that Simon Finch was Simon Warwick, and Harold Benson was not."

"That's right. He came nosing around Charlottesville, trying to see Sally. Of course, she couldn't risk meeting him. She made some excuse, and he never followed it up."

"Quince's father knew about Simon's eyes," said Henry. "He was the English lawyer who visited the Finches. He died some time ago. As far as I know, nobody else except Lord Charlton himself . . ." He stopped.

Benson said, "I wasn't really worried—not by that very clumsy attempt to push me under a bus. What scared me was the note I found in my pocket."

"Why?"

"Because it seemed to me that somebody had found out about Sally, and that it was a threat to her, not to me. I knew somebody had killed Goodman because they believed him to be Simon Warwick, and that person, I thought, was prepared to kill Sally. Anybody who had found out the truth would know that Hank must be adopted, and so couldn't inherit if Sally was dead. That's why I decided to drop the claim—like I said, no amount of money could be worth Sally's life. That's why I'm so grateful to you for preventing her from coming over here." Benson leaned forward and spoke very seriously. "Chief Superintendent, the person who murdered Ronald Goodman knows now that my wife was born Simon Warwick. I'm convinced of it. If Sally came to this country, she'd be in very great danger. You must believe me."

Henry sighed. "I do believe you," he said, "and I'm afraid I've got bad news for you."

"What bad news?"

"That cable was faked. Your wife is in England. She arrived this morning, as arranged."

Benson jumped to his feet. "Then where is she?"

"I'm afraid I don't know."

"Then you bloody well ought to know! What's a police force for?

I told you, if you didn't stop her, then you'd have to protect her—"

Henry said, "Mr. Benson, if you'd told us sooner what you've told me this morning, things would have been very different."

"You knew already! You knew that Sally was Simon Warwick, and you didn't do a damn thing about it! It's all very well for you. If it was *your* wife . . ."

Henry said, "It is, Mr. Benson."

"What?"

"My wife," Henry said, "is an exceptionally nice person. When I told her there was no way we could meet Mrs. Benson officially, she decided to go out to the airport herself. I found out just yesterday that Simon Warwick had one blue eye and one green, and my wife knew this—so when she saw your wife, she realized the truth. She telephoned me from the airport."

"And then . . .? Where is she now?"

"I wish I knew." Henry stood up. "Both our wives, Mr. Benson, seem to have disappeared."

15

The blonde girl was nervous. Emmy sensed it right away, and wondered if Sally Benson noticed it, too. Sally, however, appeared perfectly self-possessed and unaware of anything unusual.

"It really was most kind of Mr. Colby to send the car," she was saying. "I do appreciate it. Oh, may I introduce Mrs. Tibbett? She very kindly met the airplane, not knowing that Mr. Colby had made other arrangements for me." She turned to Emmy with a smile. "Well, I guess Mr. Colby will be waiting for me in his office, so if you're sure you can take the subway on to town . . ."

"Oh. Oh, no, Mrs. Benson." The blonde interrupted Sally with a nervous little laugh. "I'm afraid . . . that is, Mr. Colby asked me to meet you here, because it so happens he had to go up to town himself this morning. I'm to drive you up, and he'll meet you at your hotel. So if you—"

"Why, that's splendid," said Sally Benson. "Then we can give you a ride into London, Mrs. Tibbett. Can't we, Miss . . .?"

"Smith," said the blonde. "Deborah Smith. Well, Mrs. Benson, I don't know whether Mr. Colby—"

"I'll take the responsibility, Miss Smith," said Sally, easily. "Shall we get in the back? After you, Mrs. Tibbett."

When the small car was on its way, Sally Benson said, "Have you seen my husband, Miss Smith?"

"I . . . no. I haven't seen him myself. Of course, Mr. Colby sees him."

"How is he?"

"Well . . . Mr. Colby hasn't said, really. I expect he's all right."

Sally exchanged a brief, amused look with Emmy, as if to indicate the hopelessness of trying to extract information from Miss Smith. She said, "You haven't told me yet why you were so kind as to come out to meet me, Mrs. Tibbett. You're a friend of Ambrose Quince's, are you?"

"Yes." Emmy hesitated. She could hardly admit to being the wife of the detective who had arrested Harold Benson, and she wanted to remain anonymous as far as Miss Smith was concerned.

"I was so sorry to miss him and his wife when they were in the States," Sally said, smoothly. "Harold says he has been very helpful. I believe it was he who recommended Mr. Colby. I'm surprised he didn't tell you that I was being met at the airport, Mrs. Tibbett."

"I don't suppose he knew," said Emmy. "Your husband must have had a change of heart."

"What do you mean?" Sally's voice was cold.

Unhappily, Emmy said, "Well, you must surely know that he didn't want you to come over here. He was trying to discourage you—for your own sake."

Sally said, "Oh, Harry is such a worrier. I'm sure nothing can happen to me while I have Mr. Colby and Miss Smith to look after me."

Was there an ironic undertone? Emmy could not be sure. She was, however, convinced that if Sally Benson suspected anybody of bad faith or evil intentions, it was Emmy Tibbett. Perhaps I'm being ridiculous, Emmy thought. Why shouldn't all this be perfectly aboveboard and straightforward? What more natural than that Mr. Colby should order a car, and send his secretary, Miss Smith, to meet Mrs. Benson. Sally certainly appeared to see nothing suspicious in the setup. Emmy, however, had the advantage of being on home ground. Living in London, she knew that it was unlikely that Ambrose would have recommended a suburban solicitor to act in a murder case; and she had taken good note of 61, High Street, Hounslow. The ground floor was a grocery shop, and there had been no brass plate on the street door to indicate offices above. So long as I stick to her, Emmy thought, they can't very well murder her. Of course, they could kill us both. Emmy wished that she were braver.

By now, the car was negotiating Hammersmith Bridge, and Sally Benson said, "We seem to be getting into the city. That must be the river Thames. I've always wanted to see it. You must tell us where you'd like to be dropped off, Mrs. Tibbett."

"I . . . I was actually going up to the West End," said Emmy, hoping that she was guessing right. "Which hotel are you staying at?"

"The . . . the London Metropole, isn't it, Miss Smith?"

Good, Emmy thought. I guessed right.

The blonde cleared her throat and said, "As a matter of fact, no, Mrs. Benson. There was a mix-up about the reservation. You're booked at the Sloane Palace. So we'll drop you off in Sloane Square, Mrs. Tibbett, and you can get a cab from there."

Dammit, Emmy thought. Can't change my mind now. Aloud, she said, "That'll be fine. Thank you."

It was a quarter to one when the green Morris pulled up beside the taxi rank in Sloane Square. Sally Benson leaned across Emmy to open the door, and said, "Well, goodbye, Mrs. Tibbett. It has been so nice meeting you. I hope we may see each other again when this dreadful business has been cleared up. Thank you for your kindness."

Emmy muttered something about it being a pleasure, got out of the car, and hailed the leading cab on the rank.

"Where to, m'am?"

"I don't . . . just a minute . . ."

"Make up your mind, luv," said the cabby.

The green Morris, still distinguishable in the swirl of traffic, had completed the half circuit of Sloane Square, and turned up Sloane Street. Not in the direction of the Sloane Palace Hotel.

"Go up Sloane Street," said Emmy. "Quickly." She could not quite bring herself to say, "Follow that car." Instead, she said, "You see that green Morris stopped at the lights? Just go where it goes. My friends are showing me the way to . . ."

The driver sighed noisily. "Follow that car. Why can't you say so? Wot are you, then—private detective? Divorce case, is it?"

"Just follow the green Morris," said Emmy.

The cabby winked at her in the mirror. "I get it, I get it. No names, no pack drill." The Morris turned right into Knightsbridge. "Goin' up west, by the look of it."

The Morris took the underpass to avoid Hyde Park Corner, emerged into Piccadilly, and soon pulled over into the left-hand stream. Then it took a left turn and threaded its way through the maze of fashionable streets to pull up outside a giant new American hotel that had recently opened its doors in the popular tourist area between Piccadilly and Bond Street.

"Stop here!" Emmy said. She jumped out, paid the cabby and joined a group of German-speaking shoppers who were volubly comparing prices displayed in various enticing boutique windows. Protected from view by the crowd, Emmy saw Sally Benson get out of the green Morris at the entrance of the London Metropole Hotel. Deborah Smith did not get out, and Emmy could imagine her explaining that it was impossible to do more than drop her passenger at the door. Indeed, the doorman from the hotel had already unloaded Sally's suitcase and was indicating to the Morris that it should vacate the space outside the hotel entrance. The Morris drove away, and Sally Benson went into the hotel.

After a momentary hesitation, Emmy decided to follow her. There was plenty of coming and going through the big swing doors of the Metropole, and Emmy reckoned that she could slip in unobserved, see what Mrs. Benson was doing and if anybody was meeting her, and then telephone Henry. She was uncomfortably aware that she had not met any of the characters in the Simon Warwick drama, but only knew of them by name and from Henry's description. And neither had Sally Benson. Denton Westbury, Bertram Hamstone, even Sir Percy Crumble himself could introduce himself as Mr. Reginald Colby, and neither Sally Benson nor Emmy Tibbett would be any the wiser. Emmy took a deep breath and went through the door into the lobby, effectively disguised by a party of Indian ladies in bright saris, who carried armfuls of bulging paper bags from Marks and Spencer.

Sally Benson's suitcase and hand baggage had been neatly stacked beside the reception desk, and she herself was walking up to the desk, obviously with the intention of checking in, when a man—whose back was turned to Emmy—stepped out from behind a pillar and said something to Sally, apparently introducing himself. Sally turned and looked up to him with an attractive smile, and Emmy shrank back, feeling sure that she must have been spotted—but apparently not. Sally Benson nodded approval, presumably to some suggestion made by the man, and allowed herself to be led away to a quieter corner of the big lobby, where exhausted bargain hunters were relaxing in comfortable chairs and refreshing themselves with drinks from a bar.

149

Emmy edged closer, still trying to keep within the protective camouflage of the crowd. The man escorted Mrs. Benson to a table, made sure that she was comfortably seated, and then evidently volunteered to go and get her a drink. Emmy could see that Sally was agreeing to the idea gratefully. The man straightened, and turned away from Sally to face Emmy. It was Ambrose Quince.

At the same moment, Sally looked up. Emmy could not see her eyes, for she had put her big dark glasses on again, but they must have looked straight into Emmy's face, because she waved, stood up, and called, "Why, Mrs. Tibbett!"—and then, to Ambrose, "Mr. Colby, you must meet Mrs. Tibbett. She was at the airport this morning."

There was nothing Emmy could do. She stepped out of the crowded foyer into the bar area.

Ambrose Quince said, "How nice to see you again, Mrs. Tibbett"—and then, "So Scotland Yard arranged a reception committee for Mrs. Benson, did it? Isn't that a little unusual?"

Sally Benson said, sharply, "Scotland Yard?"

"Why, yes." Ambrose smiled. "Didn't Mrs. Tibbett tell you that her husband is the chief superintendent who arrested your husband?"

Emmy said, weakly, "Mr. Quince . . . I had no idea . . ." Words failed her.

Sally Benson was looking from one to the other of them in bewilderment. She said, "Mr. Colby . . ."

"I'm afraid," said Ambrose, "that there has been a slight misunderstanding, entirely due to Colby's imbecile secretary. For a start, she got the hotel booking muddled up, and tried to take Mrs. Benson to the Sloane Palace—or so I understand. Then she told Mrs. Benson that Reggie was going to meet her here, when she knew perfectly well that Reggie couldn't get away till later. I happened to see him at the Law Courts a little while ago, and so I volunteered to come along in his place to greet this charming lady."

"But—" Sally began.

Ambrose said, "This place is bedlam, isn't it? Can't hear yourself think. I did realize that you had misunderstood me, Mrs. Benson, and that you thought I was Reggie Colby—but it seemed only human to get you a drink before I set you right. Will you join us, Mrs. Tibbett? I haven't long, I'm afraid. I have to get back to court."

"Thank you, Mr. Quince," said Emmy. "May I have a dry sherry?" She sat down at the table, and Ambrose made his way to the bar.

Ambrose Quince. It couldn't be true. He wasn't even on Henry's list of suspects. He was an executor of the will, he stood to gain nothing, one way or the other. It didn't make sense. Emmy told herself not to be idiotic. Ambrose was simply here, as a friend of Mr. Colby's, to welcome Sally and buy her a drink. Colby's secretary had made a muddle over the name of the hotel. Soon Reginald Colby himself would arrive to take care of Sally.

Emmy began to feel extremely silly. She didn't like to think of the anxiety she must have caused Henry. Her car was abandoned in a garage at Heathrow Airport. She had been the first person to identify Simon Warwick, but that was all she had done. And meanwhile, Sally Benson was looking at her with suspicious hostility, as she had every right to do. Emmy stood up.

"Please excuse me for a moment, Mrs. Benson. I have to make a phone call. I'll be back."

There was a row of telephone booths at the far end of the lobby. Emmy made her way over to them through the ever-increasing lunchtime crowds, searched in her purse for the right coins, and dialed Scotland Yard.

"Henry . . . this is me."

"Thank God for that. Where are you?"

"Henry, I've been an utter fool."

"Never mind that. Where are you, and where is Mrs. Benson?"

"We're both at the London Metropole. I got a ride into town with her from the airport."

"From Hounslow High Street, you mean, don't you?"

Oh God, he even knows about that. "Well, yes. The secretary was there to meet us, and she drove us in."

"What secretary?"

"Deborah Smith. Mr. Colby's secretary. Ambrose Quince says—"

"Ambrose Quince?"

Oh, do listen, Henry. Everything is perfectly all right. Mr. Colby—Benson's lawyer—couldn't get away to meet Sally, so Ambrose came along here in his place—"

Henry said, "You mean that you and Mrs. Benson and Ambrose Quince are all together at the Metropole?"

"Yes. In the lobby bar. Ambrose just went off to get us a drink."

"Has anything been said about Sally Benson being Simon Warwick?"

"No, of course not. And she's wearing dark glasses, so nobody can see—"

"Okay," said Henry. "Stay where you are. Keep up a jolly conversation. For God's sake, don't lose her. Don't let her out of your sight. I'll be right over."

"But Henry—"

"Just do as I say." The line went dead.

Mystified, Emmy made her way back through the polyglot crowd to the bar area. The table where she had been sitting was now occupied by a party of massive Dutch ladies and gentlemen, drinking beer. Of Sally Benson and Ambrose Quince, there was no sign at all. Then Ambrose emerged from the crowd of people clustered round the bar, carrying three glasses of sherry with some difficulty. He and Emmy faced each other.

Ambrose said, "Where's Mrs. Benson?"

"I don't know. I went to make a phone call. She was sitting at the table when I last saw her."

Ambrose relaxed. "I expect she's just gone to freshen up, in the American euphemism. Meanwhile, she's lost us our table. Ah, those people seem to be going. Grab yourself a chair, quick."

Ten minutes later, Sally Benson's drink was still untasted on the table and Ambrose had gone back to the bar to get a refill for his own glass—when Henry arrived, followed at a discreet distance by Inspector Reynolds. He came up to Emmy and said, "Where are they?"

Emmy said, "Ambrose is getting a drink at the bar, and Sally is presumably in the ladies'."

"Presumably? You don't know?"

"Oh, Henry, she'll be back in a moment. She went off while Ambrose was buying drinks and I was telephoning to you. After all, she's just had a long journey. It's perfectly natural for her to—"

Henry said, "So she's been gone almost a quarter of an hour?"

"Yes, but—"

"There's a ladies' room just over there. Go and see if you can find her."

Sally Benson was not in the ladies' room. Emmy came back to report the fact, and found Henry looking grim, and Ambrose Quince amused.

"It's not funny, Mr. Quince," Henry said. "Somebody could

easily have approached her while you and Emmy were both out of the way."

"My dear fellow," Ambrose said, "why on earth should anybody do that? Maybe she decided to check in and go up to her room."

"We'll see," Henry said. He beckoned to Derek Reynolds, who came over to the table. The two men exchanged a quiet word, and then Reynolds went over to the reception desk. Emmy could see him talking to the clerk and producing his identification card.

Ambrose said, "What *is* all this, Tibbett?"

"I'm anxious to talk to this elusive young woman," said Henry. "Just as you were in Charlottesville. Now she appears to have done another vanishing act."

Emmy said, "As soon as Ambrose told her I was your wife—"

"Exactly," said Henry. "I did tell you not to go to the airport. Well, there may be a simple explanation, but—" He broke off as Reynolds came back to the table.

"No sign of her, sir. She hasn't checked in or taken her key. Her baggage is at the desk, waiting to go up to her room." He paused. "I'm afraid she must have left the hotel, sir."

Henry said, "There are three exits. The main one onto Hay Street, the side one onto Bruton Square, and the garage exit into Farmer Mews at the back. You've got her description, Inspector Reynolds. Check whether any of the doormen noticed her leaving."

Reynolds reported back a few minutes later. Nobody had seen her. Sally Benson had disappeared and London had swallowed her up. "Well," said Ambrose, "I'm sorry about this, Tibbett, but I'm afraid it's your problem. I must snatch a sandwich and get back to court. Goodbye, Mrs. Tibbett. So nice . . ." He was gone.

Emmy said, "Henry, I'm terribly sorry. You were right, I should never have gone to the airport. I—"

"Don't be an idiot, darling," Henry said. "You almost certainly saved her life—for a little while, at any rate. What we must do now is find her."

"You think somebody came while Ambrose and I were both away, and persuaded her to—?"

"I think," Henry said, "that she left the hotel voluntarily, but I don't know whether she was alone or not, or where she went. Does she have our address in Chelsea?"

"No, but she knows my name. She could look us up in the phone book if she wanted to, but I can't imagine her doing it. She obviously suspected a trap of some sort when Ambrose Quince blurted out who I was. I think she disappeared just to get away from me."

"I hope you're right," Henry said.

During the afternoon, reports started coming in from the various plainclothesmen who were keeping their discreet eyes on what Henry mentally categorized as the Old Will Group.

Denton Westbury had not returned to his apartment, and so far had not been located. Sir Percy Crumble had lunched at a Mayfair restaurant and returned on foot to his office. Lady Diana Crumble and Miss Cecily Smeed had been picked up at the Down Street house by Sir Percy's chauffeur-driven Bentley at half-past two. There was a blonde woman already in the car. She appeared to be on friendly terms with both ladies. Henry remembered the social secretary, and wondered. The car had dropped Miss Smeed at the Amalgamated Textiles building where she worked, and then taken the other two women to a Chelsea art gallery, where Lady Diana appeared to be selecting a picture to buy. The detective had managed to get a photograph of the blonde, which was being rushed to the Yard.

Bertram Hamstone had left Sprott's Bank at a quarter to three, in the company of a fair girl whom the detective took to be his secretary. ("All these ruddy blondes," as Inspector Reynolds remarked.) They had taken a taxi to the Hamstone house in Saint John's Wood. A photograph was on its way now to the chief superintendent's office.

Ambrose Quince was at the Law Courts, where the Westchester divorce suit had just been concluded to the dissatisfaction of all parties except the sensational press. The detective constable who was keeping a routine eye on Quince's office building, as the site of a murder as yet unsolved, reported that Susan Benedict—whom he knew well by sight—had driven up in a taxi at half-past two, accompanied by a middle-aged lady who had a lot of packages with her, mostly purchases from Selfridge's. The two had embraced, and Susan had said, "Goodbye for now, then, mother," and gone into the building, while the taxi bore the other lady away. The constable, who could put two and two together, reckoned that Miss Benedict had taken her mother out shopping.

Meanwhile, Henry had another long telephone conversation with Mr. Reginald Colby. When it was over, he called Emmy at home.

"Well," he said, "at least we know now where Sally Benson is."

"You do? Where is she? Is she all right?"

"Depends what you mean by 'all right,'" Henry said. "There was no mystery about her leaving the hotel, after all that. Colby came and collected her while you and Quince both had your backs turned. She went with him right away, thinking she was going to see her husband. Instead, Colby took her to his office, where she is currently having hysterics."

"Hysterics?"

"Colby had to tell her, you see, that he couldn't take her to the remand center, because her husband still refused to see her. Colby is trying to persuade her to take the next plane home, and she is refusing. That's the state of play so far."

Emmy said, "Does Mr. Colby know who she really is?"

"At the moment," Henry said, "nobody knows that except you and I and Inspector Reynolds, and, I'm afraid, one other person. The question is—who is that person? Can you come round here to the office right away, darling? I've got some photographs to show you. I think we may be on the track of Miss Deborah Smith, who is most certainly not Colby's secretary. After that, I'm going round to Colby's office to talk to Mrs. Benson myself. She has to be made to see reason and get out of the country."

At half-past three, Reginald Colby again telephoned Henry Tibbett. Henry listened for a moment, and then said, "Oh, my God. No, of course it wasn't your fault. Okay. Yes, keep in touch."

Emmy, who was sitting on the other side of the desk examining a rather blurred color snapshot, said, "This isn't her, either." And then, "What's the matter, Henry?"

"The vanishing lady," Henry said grimly, "has vanished again. Left Colby's office to powder her nose and never came back. Colby's office. The one place I wasn't having watched. I thought she was safe there."

"Perhaps she's making her own way to the remand center," Emmy said. "At least she's disappeared of her own accord."

The remand center knew nothing about Mrs. Benson, then or later on. The London Metropole Hotel confirmed that she had not checked in. Her baggage was still at the reception desk. Emmy, sent home to the Tibbetts' flat in case Sally Benson should try to contact her, sat by a maddeningly silent telephone. At five o'clock, Henry called Ambrose Quince at home.

"Contact me? No, old man. I called Susan at the office before I left court—no messages. And there's been nothing here. Just a moment while I check with Rosalie . . ." His voice became faint, but still audible. "A Mrs. Benson didn't call, did she, darling?" Then, into the mouthpiece, "No, Tibbett. No word from her. Why d'you think she'd contact me?"

Henry said, "You're one of the very few people in England whom she knows. And frankly, I'm worried about her."

Ambrose said, "It's your business, of course, but I really can't see what all the fuss is about. I can't see that anybody would gain anything by harming her."

Very seriously, Henry said, "It's not that aspect that's bothering me. What I'm afraid of is that she might harm herself. Benson is being a stubborn fool for some reason, and Colby said she was really distraught. If she does get in touch with you, for heaven's sake try to find out where she is, and let me know. Try to get her to go to your house . . . I'm sure Rosalie would be good at calming her down. If she's left on her own, in this frame of mind . . . Well, keep in touch, will you?"

"Of course I will. Of course. Anything we can do. I'll tell Rosalie."

It was a few minutes before ten o'clock that night that Ambrose telephoned Henry Tibbett at his home. He was upset, and got down to the facts without preamble.

"Tibbett? She's just called. You were absolutely right. She sounded . . . no, not hysterical, but deadly calm. I think she's planning to kill herself."

"Did she tell you where she was?"

"No. I asked her several times, but she simply ignored my question. She said she wanted to thank me for my support and friendship. Goodness knows, I've done nothing for her. I suppose she just wanted to talk to somebody. She apologized for calling so late, but said she would be gone by tomorrow. I said, 'Back to America, you mean?' and she said, 'No, not to America. Just gone.' And then she hung up."

"What time was this?" Henry asked.

"Just a few minutes ago. I didn't notice exactly . . . perhaps Rosalie did . . ." More faintly: "Did you notice the exact time of that call, darling? . . . Hello, Tibbett. Rosalie says it was about eighteen minutes to ten . . . No, not a clue where from . . . except it must have been a pay box, because I heard the money drop as she pressed the button."

"That doesn't get us very far," said Henry.

"I know that. At least it shows she wasn't calling from her hotel room."

"She hasn't been back to the hotel," Henry said. "They're to let me know at once if she does. Well, thanks for letting me know, Quince. We'll do our best to find her."

"You'd better, old man," said Ambrose. "Because tomorrow may be too late."

Henry put down the telephone and stood up. "I have to go, Emmy," he said.

From the kitchen, her hands wet with washing-up water, Emmy said, "Go? Where?"

"To find Sally Benson."

16

Sally Benson stood in the dark on the flat roof of the London
Metropole Hotel, looking down at the crawling lights of toy-size
cars and taxicabs twenty stories below her. She shivered. She
knew what she had to do, but she had not imagined that it would be
as hard as this. There was nothing for it, however. She had to do it.

It had been absurdly easy to fool the hotel staff. A dark wig, a
change of clothes, a room on the top floor booked in a false name,
and no questions asked. After all, even if the police were watching
the hotel, the best they would have to go on would be a snapshot
from Harry's wallet. Nobody in England would recognize her
except Ambrose Quince, Emmy Tibbett, and Deborah Smith.

In the impersonally pretty hotel bedroom, she had written a note
for her husband. They would find it in the morning.

> Darling Harry,
> By the time you read this, I shall be dead. Believe me, my
> love, I did the only thing that would give any chance of a
> happy life in the future for you and Hank. I must explain
> everything to you. You see . . .

When she heard the light footstep on the roof behind her, she did
not turn her head at once, but stood quite still. Then she turned
round, her back to the flimsy parapet. The flat roof, under the

sparse light of a clouded half-moon, presented an eerie landscape of strange shapes—ventilators, television aerials, air-conditioning units. From behind one of the angular, huddled shapes, a figure stepped out.

Sally said, "You are very punctual."

"I always keep my appointments, Mrs. Benson."

"We have a lot to talk about, you and I. You know that I was born Simon Warwick?"

"Of course."

"I won't even ask how you found out. It doesn't matter any longer. The point is that you know. It is also vitally important for you that Lord Charlton's old will should come back into force— and soon."

The newcomer smiled in the darkness. "I shall return the compliment, Mrs. Benson, and refrain from asking you how you know that."

"By a process of deduction, of course. You wouldn't have killed Ronald Goodman if you hadn't been desperate."

"That was an unfortunate mistake. How was I to know—?"

"He shouldn't have been so greedy," said Sally. "Greedy and deceitful. I am neither. I am prepared to do a deal with you."

"Because you dare not make your claim publicly."

"It would be . . . inconvenient for me to do so. So, you see, we can help each other. I will make no claim. On the other hand, you will arrange for the Charlton Foundation to be especially generous to a certain charity. Shall we call it the Friends of Charlottesville?"

"What makes you think I can influence the foundation?"

"Your great experience," said Sally Benson, "in the setting up of phony charities. I'm making you a very generous offer. If you refuse it, I shall go to the police and tell them that you killed Ronald Goodman."

"They wouldn't believe you."

"Are you prepared to risk that? I will also make and substantiate my claim to be Simon Warwick. And as Simon Warwick, when I investigate various financial transactions concerning the affairs of the late Lord Charlton, your motive for wanting to do away with Simon Finch will become very obvious, won't it?"

"And if I agree, you are prepared to let your own husband be convicted for a murder he did not commit?"

Sally smiled. "It's hardly surprising that he doesn't want to see me, is it?"

The other stepped forward and caught her arm. "You are a devil. A cool, calculating devil."

"And quite ruthless," said Sally.

"By God, you deserve what's coming to you. You—"

They were both up against the parapet by then. The pressure on Sally's arm was becoming intolerable. Another moment, and she would be forced over the edge and into the abyss. She screamed.

The searchlight beam of a powerful torch flashed with brutal impact on the two struggling figures, and suddenly the roof was full of people. Strong hands dragged Sally's assailant away from her, and Inspector Reynolds's voice said, "Ambrose Quince, I am arresting you for the attempted murder of Mrs. Sally Benson. You are not obliged to say anything unless you wish to do so, but whatever you say will be taken down in writing and may be given in evidence."

Ambrose Quince did not have anything to say. Meekly, almost with relief, he allowed himself to be marched by Inspector Reynolds and Sergeant Hawthorn to the iron staircase that led down into the hotel. At the head of the staircase, Henry Tibbett was standing, his arms folded. Ambrose Quince lifted his head and for a long moment the two men looked at each other. Then Ambrose gave a curious half-smile and a little, congratulatory nod. And he was gone. Henry walked across the roof to Sally Benson.

"Was I all right, Mr. Tibbett?"

"I only got here for the last part," Henry said, "but what I heard was sensational. You are a very brave woman, Mrs. Benson."

Sally said, "I'd like to go down to my room now. There's a letter I want to destroy."

"A letter?"

"I wrote to Harry . . . to explain . . . that is, if our plan hadn't worked and he'd managed to kill me after all . . . I didn't want him to blame you . . ."

Henry said, "You don't seem to have had much faith in the British police, Mrs. Benson." But as he walked with her to the staircase, Henry found that he was sweating. It had been a risk, but it had been the only way.

Much later, Henry and Emmy Tibbett and Sally Benson sat drinking coffee in the Tibbetts' apartment, unraveling for Emmy's benefit the events of the preceding day.

"Why didn't you tell me the truth?" Emmy demanded, reproachfully. "Didn't you trust me?"

"Not altogether," Henry said, and then, seeing his wife's outraged face, added, "You see, darling, you're too honest. Ambrose Quince might have telephoned you, and you could have given something away. Besides, at that point I couldn't tell anybody my suspicions about him, because I had no absolute proof of anything. I couldn't possibly charge him with murdering Ronald Goodman while I had another man in custody for the same crime, and as far as Sally was concerned, he'd done nothing criminal. The only way was to set a trap for him."

"You'd better start at the beginning," Emmy said. "I'm thoroughly confused. Ambrose was the executor of the will. He didn't stand to gain or lose, one way or the other, whichever will was proven. You said so yourself."

"And thought so, at the time," Henry admitted. "However, when I found certain evidence in the Goodman murder beginning to point towards Quince, I started to ask myself if he might not have a motive, after all. Well, we've got the whole story out of Denton Westbury now. As I had begun to suspect, Quince had been cheating Lord Charlton for years over his charitable donations, the greater part of which went into Quince's own pocket. However, the Charlton Foundation was to have been the real big-time swindle.

"Westbury was to be the cover—a purely decorative figure. All he was required to do was keep his mouth shut and draw a large salary. Hamstone was too busy at Sprott's to take any active part in the foundation—he'd have been content to leave it to Quince. For personal reasons, Cecily Smeed was primarily concerned that Westbury should get the job, so even if she had suspected anything, she'd have kept quiet. And of course, the foundation would have had nothing whatsoever to do with the Crumbles or Warwick Industries.

"Certainly, a number of very respectable charities would have benefited from the Charlton fortune—but a number of others, completely phony, had already been set up by Quince in Lord Charlton's lifetime, and he had managed to get the old man's approval of them as deserving causes. Money paid into them would have found its way, by devious channels, into Quince's account. He has a very ambitious and extravagant wife, and personally I think she would have left him long ago if he hadn't promised her a handsome income once Charlton died.

"Of course, Quince had to appear eager to find Simon Warwick. Well, in a way he actually *was* eager to do so, in order to get him out

161

of the way. When he had convinced himself beyond all possible doubt that Simon Finch was Simon Warwick, that signed poor Goodman's death warrant. Quince didn't realize he was an impostor. He carefully set up Harold Benson as the obvious suspect, with motive and opportunity. However, just in case anything went wrong there, he was careful to assemble all the beneficiaries under the old will, and acquaint them with all the facts. That gave him a nice basket of red herrings. They all had motives, except Hamstone. Quince apparently didn't.

"Of course, it was Quince himself who telephoned, with an assumed American accent, to change the time of Goodman's appointment. All he had to do then was to come early to the office, let himself in through his own office and into the waiting room. Goodman was expecting him, and had no reason to be suspicious. A quick karate chop—as demonstrated by Hamstone, the ex-Commando, in all innocence—and Goodman was quickly and quietly strangled. Quince is very strong."

"I know that," said Sally ruefully, rubbing her arm.

"A copy of the *Times* laid over the dead man's face made sure that Benson wouldn't realize that Goodman was dead until he'd been in the office long enough to have committed the crime himself."

Emmy said, "Quince was lucky that Goodman had a paper with him."

"But he didn't," Henry said.

"I thought the girl—the secretary—said that he did."

"So she did. But she now admits that she really didn't notice one way or the other, but that Ambrose pretty well put the words into her mouth while waiting for us to arrive at the office. Since then, thinking about it, she has realized that Goodman *didn't* have a paper, because the thought crossed her mind that he'd have nothing to read in the waiting room but some old magazines. She asked Ambrose if she should come to me and change her story, and Ambrose, of course, forbade her to do any such thing. In fact, it was the business of the newspapers that first put me onto Quince."

"How was that?" Sally asked.

"Well, Quince couldn't bank on Goodman bringing a paper with him. On the other hand, he couldn't use his own—he bought one every morning from the same newsvendor, and he had to be able to produce it. He particularly wanted to keep exactly to his normal routine that morning. But he needed a second copy of the *Times*. So he did the obvious thing—he brought his copy from home.

When I went to talk to his wife that day, she wanted to look something up in the *Times*, but couldn't find the paper; yesterday, on the other hand, when she wanted to check something, the paper was in its usual place, right by the telephone. It was a very small thing, but it made me wonder. If Quince had taken the paper from home, and bought another one, and if Susan Benedict's evidence was right, then there should have been *three* copies of the paper in Quince's office. But there were only two."

"It must have been an awful blow to Quince when he found he'd killed the wrong man," Emmy said.

"It must indeed," Henry agreed. "Worse than that, he knew that if Harold Benson could make good his claim, a second murder would get him nowhere. Goodman had been unmarried, with no legitimate child. Quince assumed that young Harold was Benson's natural son, and so would inherit even if his father were to die. He explained to Westbury that only if Benson's claim could be disproved definitely, or if Benson withdrew it, could they be sure that the foundation would go ahead. Westbury, who is not very bright, decided to take matters into his own hands and try to frighten Benson into withdrawing his claim by an apparent murder attempt and a threatening note. He wasn't to know that his ridiculous ploy would succeed, because Harold Benson interpreted it as a threat to Sally."

"But in the end, Quince found out who I was," Sally said. "How could he have done that?"

"He knew as soon as he heard about your strange eye coloring," Henry said.

"But how?"

"I remembered," Henry said, "that the Quinces had visited your home in Charlottesville. I telephoned there this evening and spoke to your maid, Bettina. She confirmed that there's a big color photograph of you in the house."

"But that's in Harry's study! What was he doing in there?"

"Talking to Bettina, apparently. Rosalie, his wife, didn't go in there and so didn't see the picture. Quince remembered your eye coloring—it's very striking, after all—but thought no more about it until his wife came and told him about my conversation with her and Lady Diana. It made you an immediate candidate for murder."

Sally frowned, and then said, "Of course. If I was Simon Warwick, then Hank would have to be adopted, and not eligible to inherit."

"Exactly. No wonder your husband wanted to keep you away

from England. Knowing that he himself hadn't killed Goodman, he knew there was a murderer at large."

"How did Quince manage the telegram from Charlottesville?" Emmy asked.

"Not difficult. He knew Sally's maid, Bettina. He called her, posing as Benson's English lawyer. Having made sure that Sally had already left home, he spun a story that Sally wanted Bettina to send a cable for her, as she had changed her plans. Bettina believed him. He thought he had arranged matters so that if Sally disappeared, she wouldn't be missed for several days, on either side of the Atlantic."

Sally shivered. "And I would have disappeared, permanently, if it hadn't been for Emmy."

Emmy said, "So I suppose Miss Deborah Smith was Susan Benedict?"

"Right," Henry said. "She was besotted about Quince, and would have done anything he told her to. She swears she had no idea she was getting involved in a murder plot. She says Quince put it to her as some sort of practical joke, and I'm inclined to believe her. Her job was to pose as Colby's secretary, arrange the hire car—Quince couldn't risk her going to the airport and perhaps being recognized—and then pick Sally up at the phony address in Hounslow and deposit her at the London Metropole, where Quince, posing as Colby, would take over. After the murder, of course, she would have been up to her neck in it as an accessory before the fact. She wouldn't have dared open her mouth."

Emmy said, "Poor Susan. She looked completely flummoxed when she saw me with Sally. She made a gallant attempt to get rid of me in Sloane Square."

Sally said, "Yes, she told Emmy we were heading for someplace called the Sloane Palace Hotel, so that Emmy wouldn't have an excuse for riding with us any longer. Then, as soon as Emmy had gotten out of the car, she conveniently remembered that I was booked at the Metropole after all. It was clever of you to follow us," she added, to Emmy.

"Not clever," said Emmy. "Just desperate. I saw that the car wasn't headed for the Sloane Palace, and I was darned certain that Mr. Colby's office wasn't over a grocery shop in Hounslow. But then, in the hotel, it all seemed so reasonable—and of course I didn't suspect Ambrose Quince for a moment . . ."

"I did," said Sally. "First, there was the business about the hotel. Then, although he passed it off as a misunderstanding, he definitely introduced himself as Reginald Colby. We were to have a drink and then drive down to the remand center. Why didn't I just leave my cases, he said. No point in bothering to check in right away. For a moment, I thought you might have been somehow in on the plot, too, Emmy. Believe me, I got out of that Metropole Hotel the very first moment I could."

"When the real Mr. Colby arrived?" Emmy said.

"No Mr. Colby arrived," said Sally. "I just hightailed it out of there when neither of you was looking."

"Then where did you go?" Emmy asked.

Henry and Sally exchanged a broad grin. Sally said, "Scotland Yard, of course. Where else? Quince made a bad mistake, telling me who you were. He told me at the same time the name of the police officer in charge of Harry's case. I grabbed a cab, drove to Scotland Yard and asked for Chief Superintendent Tibbett."

"So all that time . . . when I was so worried about you . . ." Emmy was almost speechless.

"Yes," said Henry. "She was right next door, being entertained by Inspector Reynolds. And neither hysterical nor suicidal, I need hardly add. Of course, I had spoken to Colby and found out that he never asked Ambrose Quince to meet Sally at the hotel—nor had he had time to go there himself. He agreed to cooperate by putting through a call to me, when I knew you would be in the office, giving me a thoroughly mendacious account of Sally's second disappearance." Henry smiled at Emmy. "I've said I'm sorry, darling, but I couldn't risk the danger that—believing Quince to be innocent—you might give something away. I was setting up a rather elaborate trap, you see."

Emmy sighed, in mock resignation. "All right. I know I'm a rotten actress and a rotten liar."

"Whereas Sally," said Henry, "is magnificent as both."

"How did you work it?" Emmy asked.

"Very simply. It just meant that Sally had to risk her life."

"Oh, don't be so melodramatic," Sally said. "I knew that roof was knee-deep in cops."

"Then why did you write that letter to your husband?"

Sally made a face, and laughed. "All right. Touché. But I was never really in any danger—was I?"

"I'd prefer not to answer that question," Henry said. "Let's just be thankful that it all happened as planned."

"But, Henry," Emmy protested, "Quince rang you from Ealing only a few minutes before—"

"A very old trick," Henry said. "He pretended to ask Rosalie something in the background, to make me think he was at home. Actually, of course, he was already somewhere very close to the Metropole. I don't know exactly where, and it's not important. As soon as he called, I knew that we had him.

"You see, Sally had telephoned him—but much earlier on. She was perfectly calm and didn't threaten suicide at all. What she did was to make a date to meet him at the Metropole at ten o'clock, to discuss making a deal over the inheritance. I had taken care to make him think that I thought Sally was on the point of committing suicide. I gave him just the chance he needed."

"That's why he insisted on my going up to the hotel roof," Sally put in. "I had suggested meeting in my room, but he was adamant. He said the roof was the only place where we could be sure of complete privacy and secrecy. Henry and I both knew then that he would try to kill me." She shivered.

Henry said, "I had guessed that his original plan—which Emmy fortunately wrecked—was to stage a suicide for Sally. And now it seemed to be playing right into his hands. Sally Benson falls to her death from the hotel roof, an obvious suicide, as predicted by Ambrose Quince, who has been cooperating so closely with Scotland Yard. Ambrose would have been well on his way home long before the hubbub surrounding Sally's death had subsided. His wife, who in fact has been persuaded to spend the evening at her mother's home, will say truthfully that Ambrose was at home all evening, if anybody asks her—which is highly unlikely.

"Once Sally's body had been discovered, of course, somebody—perhaps even Quince himself, but more likely he would have left it to the Crumbles—would have spotted the truth, that Sally had been born Simon Warwick. The hospital records of the operation would have been traced. Identity as Simon Warwick would have been proved, and Simon Warwick would have been good and dead. His, or her, adopted son wouldn't have been eligible to inherit. Everything would have again been exactly as Ambrose Quince had arranged it, before Lord Charlton had the bizarre idea of looking for his long-lost nephew."

Emmy said, "When I was in your office, I saw some sort of report about Susan Benedict and her mother . . ."

Henry laughed. "That was a very delicate touch, to account for Susan's absence from the office. Her unsuspecting mama was lured up from Hampshire, sent off to shop at Selfridge's, and picked up by Susan after she had done her delivery job to the Metropole.

Poor Ambrose. He really believed he had thought of everything. I'm almost sorry for him. I'm rather glad I've had to disqualify myself from the case on the grounds that the accused is—or was—an acquaintance of mine." Henry yawned. "Good heavens, it's three o'clock. I'm off to bed. Got a heavy day tomorrow."

"I thought you were off the case," Emmy said.

"I meant," said Henry, "that tomorrow I have to set in motion the tedious formalities which will get Sally's husband out of jail without a blemish on his character."

"Not a—?" Sally's eyes opened wide. "What about fraudulent misrepresentation?"

"After what you did tonight?" said Henry. "Forget it. I'm going to bed."

After he had gone, the two women sat in silence for a minute. Sally stirred her coffee and stared at the embers of the fire. At last, Emmy said, "Well, it'll be interesting to see what the lawyers make of your claim."

Sally said nothing. Emmy went on, "I don't see how they can throw it out. You *are* Simon Warwick. You are the rightful heir, no matter what sex you are. And your son—"

Slowly, Sally said, "I won't be making a claim."

"You won't?"

There was a long silence. Then Sally said, "Emmy, you're a woman."

"Of course I am."

"You've always been one. You don't know what it was like . . . trying to pretend to be a man."

"That's all over now," Emmy said.

"It wouldn't be, if I made a claim."

"But—"

"Don't you see?" Sally said. "I've been so lucky. I've made my new life. I have a husband and a son, and I love them both very much. I have a place in the scheme of things. I'm just so ashamed that I let Harry come over here and do what he did. How could it possibly help Hank or Harry or me to destroy everything we've worked so hard to build up—just for money? Do you understand?"

"I think so," said Emmy. "I understand as much as anybody could."

"You understand," said Sally Benson, "because you're a woman. Like me." Another silence. Then she smiled. "I can't think what Harry will say when I tell him. You know what men are like."

Epilogue

From the *Times*, London.

Today, in the Chancery Division of the High Court, judgement was given to allow the executor of the will of the late Baron Charlton to presume the individual known as Simon Warwick to be legally dead. This decision, which was not contested by any party, means that the late Lord Charlton's fortune will go to charity, apart from certain personal bequests. A body known as the Charlton Foundation, to be headed by the executor of the will, Mr. Bertram Hamstone, will administer the Fund and nominate the charities which will benefit. It is understood that a substantial amount of money will be donated for research into the problems, both medical and psychological, of trans-sexualism.